Kiss Shot

Carolyn Elizabeth writes some of the best adrenaline-racing action packed lesfic novels and this was another to add to her list.

-Natalie T., *NetGalley*

Kiss Shot by Carolyn Elizabeth is a fast-paced adventure novel with an intricate plot, striking characters, and a slow-burn romance between two unlikely characters.

-Betty H., *NetGalley*

...is a slow burn romance packed inside a flash bang crime thriller.

-*The Lesbian Review*

The Raven and the Banshee

The Raven and the Banshee is a great adventure set in the 1700s that brought back a lot of good memories of the old swashbuckler movies I loved as a kid—but with two female leads which is even better. I don't want to give the story away, suffice to say that there's lots of drama, lots of action, lots of betrayal, lots of brooding, lots of romance. As with Ms. Elizabeth's other novels, her main characters are engaging and well rounded and even the secondary characters felt real and fleshed out.

-*To Be Read Book Reviews*

Everything I hoped it would be... swashbuckling revenge tale with a second-chance romance to die for!! Amazing. Loved it. Bought the book!! I was looking forward to this novel since it was announced, and always fear that expectations may be too high, but not a problem; Elizabeth knocks this out of the park.

-Andi K., *NetGalley*

The Other Side of Forestlands Lake

Elizabeth (*Gallows Humor*) delivers her signature blend of lesbian romance and murder in this suspenseful outing. Paranormal YA author Willa Dunn steps into her own ghost story when she returns to her childhood summer home at Forestlands Lake. She's hoping to work on her next book and reconnect with her half-sister, rebellious teenager Nicole, but her plans are derailed by a series of spectral visitations. When Nicole gets drunk and almost drowns in the lake, Willa's childhood sweetheart, Lee Chandler, saves her. Lee, now the director of a summer camp for LGBTQ youth, and her daughter, Maggie, join together with Willa and Nicole to investigate the haunting. Between ghostly possessions and cryptic conversations with mysterious neighbors, Willa and Lee rekindle the flame that was barely allowed to flicker back when they were both closeted teens. Though the story hits some speed bumps trying to juggle the tense mystery and the lighthearted romance, the charming characters will draw in readers, and the plot ultimately hangs together nicely. Fans of romantic suspense are sure to be pleased.

-Publishers Weekly

The author uses great descriptions and innocuous little details to give the community surrounding the lake a disturbing personality. This is a nice juxtaposition with the giddiness Willa and Lee feel over being reunited. I enjoyed losing myself in a paranormal story. I'm pretty set in my ways about sticking to the romance genre, but this was a nice change of pace. The book is well paced, and it's spooky enough to raise the hair on the back of your neck without making you need to sleep with the lights on.

-The Lesbian Review

It took only one book by Carolyn Elizabeth for me to decide that she was a must-read author. This is her third and it proves true again. I love Elizabeth's stories but even if I didn't, I'd read her books for the characters. She makes me fall in love with all of them.

There are many layers to this book, and so we don't get one mystery but two. Well-thought, complex and thrilling mysteries. Everything came as a surprise yet still made complete sense (in a paranormal way).

Carolyn Elizabeth is proving that she could write any genre and I'd want to read it. In this book, you get romance, paranormal and mystery all in one, with each element being as important and as well-crafted.

-Les Rêveur

Dirt Nap

This is a perfect sequel to *Gallows Humor* and met all of my... high expectations. Sometimes sequels can be disappointing, but not this one. We have the same mystery, intrigue, and romance that we found in the first book. Corey, Thayer, and all the secondary characters are just as likable and easy to connect with. The romance is still as sweet, and it was fun seeing the two grow together through all the trials they had to endure. It was also fun meeting a few new characters and watching them develop. Ms. Elizabeth not only has the knowledge she needs in pathology and medicine for this story, she also shines in character development. This is what makes both of these books so great.

-Betty H., NetGalley

I must admit that this is the second time that I was blown away with this author's captivating writing style. She has really outdone herself with this story because she gave me a riveting romantic thriller that has so many entertaining and laugh-out-loud moments embedded within it. This story kept me glued to my Kindle and hungry for more priceless wisecracks from Corey and Thayer. Even though Carolyn Elizabeth did a wonderful job of filling in some of the details and facts from her first book, I would strongly advise you to read *Gallows Humor* before you read this story so that you would get to know more about these lovely characters.

Gallows Humor

At this very moment, my coffee cup is raised in Carolyn Elizabeth's honor because she gave me the perfect blend of an angst-filled, budding romance with endless humor and an enthralling murder mystery that kept me up way past my bedtime. I still can't get over the fact that this story is her debut novel because Carolyn Elizabeth has knocked my fluffy bedroom socks off with her flawless writing and the witty and entertaining dialogue between the characters along with the vivid descriptions of the Jackson City Memorial Hospital and environs.

If you're looking for a story that will keep you on the edge of your seat and have you doubled over with laughter, then this is definitely the story for you!

The Heart of the Banshee

Carolyn Elizabeth

About the Author

Carolyn Elizabeth is a Goldie Award-winning author of seven genre-crossing books filled with action, mystery, humor and romance.

When not writing—which is often—she's working full-time for the Ontario Institute for Cancer Research, parenting two young sons, and becoming a better version of herself every day.

The Heart of the Banshee

Carolyn Elizabeth

BELLA
BOOKS

2023

First Edition - 2023

Editor: Ann Roberts
Cover Designer: Kayla Mancuso

ISBN: 978-1-64247-459-6

Acknowledgments

Thank you to Bella Books and my editor, Ann Roberts, for helping me get another one across the finish line. Your support and encouragement keep me going.

Heartfelt thanks to all our reviewers who show their love of Sapphic stories by reading the books, engaging with authors, and sharing their thoughts online. We couldn't do it without them.

Thank you to the readers who picked up my first bonkers Sapphic pirate adventure, *The Raven and the Banshee*, and made it my most popular book. This one is for them.

CHAPTER ONE

Julia Farrow slipped the fingerless leather gloves over her hands, snugging them past her wrists and tightening the laces across the back with one hand and her teeth. She'd gotten quite good at that part and was more than a little grateful that with the gloves, her weapons training sessions with Jack Massey, quartermaster of the *Banshee*, no longer ended early due to her bleeding palms. She smiled to herself, recalling the unexpected trouble she and Branna ran into the day she had purchased them.

While the danger had been real and she never looked forward to Branna fighting, she was pleased to have made a new friend in the young street urchin Henry, who now followed her around every chance he got. The arrangement Branna had made with Josiah Coombs, a former agent of Captain Cyrus Jagger, to be her eyes and ears in and around Nassau had been working out even better than she'd hoped.

She really ought to make more of an effort to be less surprised. With Branna, the unexpected occurred far too frequently for it to even be considered *unexpected*. This was her life now, the one she had agreed to when she signed her name to the *Banshee*'s Articles and became the ship's newest officer. Well, she hadn't signed in blood exactly and Branna had been clear she could change her mind at any time, but she wanted to do this. She was determined, however foolishly, to share this life with Branna.

She curled her fingers, stretching the leather. She would have thought her hands were tough enough from sailing, but the braided leather grip of her cutlass was an entirely new assault on her palms to which she hadn't yet grown accustomed.

The courtyard of Travers Trading Post at the port of Nassau was quiet this early. Genevieve Travers, owner and operator, had bustled around at dawn collecting glasses and emptying ash cans, and left a mug of coffee for Julia as was her custom this past week while Julia used the space to train for her new position as purser aboard the *Banshee*.

She drew her cutlass from the scabbard at her hip and began working through a series of warmup exercises while waiting for Jack. She enjoyed the feel of her strengthening muscles, warming and loosening with the movements, which a week ago was so very foreign to her and now something to which she looked forward.

"I was told I'd find you here."

Julia whirled at the deep rumbling voice to find a large, dark-skinned man in the entryway, a short sword in each hand, and her heart rate picked up. Caught off guard, again, but only for a moment. She breathed deeply and squared her shoulders. "Are you here to fight me?"

He crossed the courtyard slowly, rotating the swords around as he approached. "I'm afraid so."

"Afraid?" She sidestepped, keeping herself out of range and keeping a table between them, her lip twitching into a teasing smile. "Of me?"

He barked a laugh. "Best hope that wee blade of yours is as sharp as your tongue."

"You're about to find out, sir."

Julia kicked a chair, sending it sliding hard into his knees. He grunted, staggering enough at the contact that Julia had him on his heels as she rounded the table and sent a slashing cut to his neck. He parried, forced back another step into a table behind, catching him behind the knees, unbalancing him further, and allowing her another opening.

Julia controlled her breathing like she'd practiced and worked everything she had learned in the past week, as well as a few improvised moves that just felt right. She couldn't rely on strength to beat opponents and Jack had encouraged her to be creative.

She stayed on the offensive, forcing him to use both blades to fend her off as she slashed and cut from across and below, making sure to never overcommit and leave herself open to counterattack.

She knew he was toying with her. It had only been a week, and while she was a quick study, she had a lot to learn. He could have easily skewered her through the heart whenever he wanted, but he was putting her through her paces instead. She was willing to take whatever advantage he gave her.

She couldn't keep it up, though. He was too big and too strong, and she was tiring quickly. She sent a flurry of crosscuts to his midsection before darting away, putting another table between them and allowing herself a few moments to rest. She was breathing hard and sweating harder. So was he.

He mopped across his bald head with the back of his left arm and sucked in a breath to speak. "I underestimated you. I thought this would be over much quicker."

Julia allowed herself a small smile of satisfaction. "You can yield anytime."

He smiled apologetically. "I cannot, miss. I have my orders."

"What? Whose ord—bugger!"

He closed the distance in two long strides, using his much-greater height to rain chopping strikes down on her with both blades.

Iron against iron clanged a staccato beat as all Julia could do was raise her blade to take the blows, absorbing each impact with the quickly exhausting muscles of her shoulders and back. She had to move.

The next time their blades clashed, she twisted her hips and shoulders to the left, throwing his blade off and forcing him to step wide to keep his balance. She tucked and rolled between his splayed legs, coming up behind him onto her feet and twisting around into a powerful crosscut to his back that he barely blocked and not before her blade sliced his shirt open.

His eyes went wide. "Bloody hell!"

Julia sucked in a shocked breath at how close she came to severing his spine and hesitated. He took the opportunity to bring his right sword down sharply on her blade near the hilt, knocking it from her hand with a clatter while his left thrust out, the point stopping mere inches from her throat, forcing her back against a table.

Julia threw her hands behind her, groping for the table to keep from falling and closed her eyes. "I yield."

"Are you all right, miss?" Nat Hooper, the *Banshee*'s bosun moved his swords to one hand and gripped her shoulder.

Julia cracked an eye and grinned. "I had you, Nat."

"Aye, miss," he agreed and helped her straighten off the table. "You may be right."

"*May* be?" Julia dragged the back of her sleeve across her forehead to wipe sweat from her eyes. She collected her cutlass and sheathed it, then stuck her entire hand through the hole in the back of his shirt.

"Quite impressive, Julia!" Genevieve called from nearby where she'd apparently been watching. She had two large tankards of ale she held out to them. "I had no idea how far you've come. Branna will be pleased."

Julia took the ale and guzzled some in a fashion that would have her mother turning over in her grave at her ill manners. "Speaking of our dear Captain. Did she send you?"

Nat shrugged shyly. "Aye, miss. She wants to know if you could handle yourself against a much larger threat."

"Does she now?" Julia's brows rose. "And what will you be telling her, Mr. Hooper?"

"That she needn't worry so much, miss."

Julia hid her smile behind another drink of ale.

"Oy!"

They all turned at the shout from the entryway to see Gus scowling, hands on hips.

"We're waitin' on you lot," he barked and hooked a thumb over his shoulder. "Tide's turnin' now. Captain's ready to go."

Julia's heart beat hard with a jolt of excitement. It was time. She was as prepared as she was going to get in the time they had. Her life, repaired and restored, just like the *Banshee*, started now.

"Fair winds!" Genevieve called before going back to her work.

A week of nonstop intense training with Jack, and Branna sent Nat to test her. Julia was both annoyed with Branna and pleased with herself. She knew she didn't really beat him. He could have ended that fight anytime. Nevertheless, she held her own and that was a tremendous accomplishment. She didn't need anyone to tell her that, but she'd be lying if she said she didn't hope Nat spoke well of her to Branna.

Her distracted thoughts led her to slow, dropping behind Nat and Gus as they wended their way down the busy dock toward the boat waiting to take them out to the ship and get underway.

The harbor was always busy at high tide with ships both coming and going, loading and unloading. Merchants, sailors, dockworkers, and errand boys crowded the limited space, dodging each other and crates of cargo and supplies stacked haphazardly on every available flat surface.

She jumped out of the way of a rushing young sailor and bumped into the back of a man who appeared to be urinating off the dock. He swore and staggered around to face her.

Julia's face flamed with embarrassment, and she quickly looked away while he buttoned his stained breeches with one hand and swilled from a grimy bottle with the other.

"Watch where yer goin'," he growled, wiping his face with the back of his arm.

Julia's gaze flicked over him, and she grimaced as his rum-soaked breath and sour body odor washed over her. She knew him and he was drunker and filthier than when she'd seen him a week ago—likely having neither washed nor stopped drinking since. "Are you all right?"

He swayed. "Don' I look all right?"

She peered down to the end of the dock and could see the boat, Nat at the oars, bobbing in the water, and a very annoyed-looking Gus scanning the crowds for her.

"I'm in a bit of a hurry, Mr. Blythe, but I could take a few minutes to help—"

"Don't need no help," he slurred, his eyes narrowing. "An' how the 'ell do ya know my name?"

"We met a few days ago at the tavern. I'm Julia Far—"

"Right. Right." He wagged a greasy finger. "I 'member now. Yer Kelly's slag."

Julia took a step back at the insult. While she understood the source of his anger toward Branna, she was no longer interested in helping him unless she was helping him off the edge of the dock with her boot in his arse. She turned with a wave of her hand. "Carry on, then."

She yelped when his hand clamped hard around her right arm. She tried to pull away and his grip tightened painfully. "Let me go," she gasped, her pulse pounding with shock and a jolt of fear.

He jerked her back toward him and snarled in her ear, "Kelly ain't who ya think. She's a liar an' coward. Don' let 'er fool ya inta believin' otherwise."

Her fear quickly turned to anger at the insult to Branna and she bent her arm and twisted sharply away from him, breaking his hold. She spun back, sending her elbow into his throat, just like Jack had showed her.

Thomas Blythe gagged, clutching his neck, and staggered backward over a crate onto his arse. Julia made no move to help when he vomited all over himself.

"Well done, Julia," Gus said.

Julia rubbed her arm, still feeling the press of his hand against her skin. "How much did you see?"

"Enough." He reached for her arm. "Are you hurt?"

"I'm fine. Just a bruise. It's nothing."

Gus started them walking toward the end of the dock. "Since we're heading out, Blythe gets a reprieve, but I assure you, Branna will take care of him when we—"

"No. It was a misunderstanding."

"Branna will not see it that way."

"Don't tell her."

He stopped. "Julia, I have to tell—"

"You don't." Julia fixed him with her gaze. "I'm fine. Thomas Blythe is…"

"Is what?"

She knew the haunted look in his eyes all too well. The difference was, she had help to deal with her trauma—family, friends, financial security. And bodies to bury. She knew what happened to her crew and she could make peace with that. Without knowing what happened to the *Windswept*, Thomas Blythe would continue to suffer as if it happened just yesterday. Julia cleared her throat, tears threatening. "In a lot of pain. Pain I understand and I don't want to add to."

Gus sighed heavily and nodded. "This may come back around, Julia. I hope you're prepared if it does."

"I know. I'll handle it."

CHAPTER TWO

Six Days Earlier

Branna Kelly, captain of Nassau's mercenary ship *Banshee*, and Julia Farrow, the ship's newest officer, walked quietly hand in hand back to Travers Trading Post after their intimate night on the *Banshee*.

Last night Branna had offered Julia a place on her crew as the ship's new purser and Julia, for better or worse, had accepted. Her gaze flicked to Julia who seemed relaxed and happy. Branna wanted their life to continue together, with Julia sailing with her as an officer on the *Banshee*, but she couldn't quite settle the part of her that felt like she was making a mistake. That this may very well end badly for them both.

She shook off her sense of foreboding. All she could be was honest, tell Julia how she felt, and what may lie ahead for them. She had to trust that Julia would make the decision that was right for her.

Genevieve and Merriam Beeson, Gen's right hand, were at a table in the courtyard having breakfast when Julia and Branna slunk back in looking bed tousled and happily exhausted.

Branna's long black hair was loose from its customary braid and her shirt was buttoned wrong. Julia's still-growing blond waves needed untangling and her skirt may have been on backward. Branna gripped Julia's hand and pulled them to a stop.

Genevieve eyed them both with a raised brow. "Well, you two look...refreshed."

"Um..." Branna glanced at Julia who was working hard to cover a laugh. "We were just, uh, we had to just..."

"Save yer strength, Kelly. We know what ya were *just*," Merri said and popped a piece of fruit in her mouth.

"We had some things to work out," Julia said, and she beamed at Branna before looking at their friends.

"Uh-huh," Merri mumbled around her food. "Speaking of working out, Kelly, are we training today?"

"No." Branna straightened and turned all business. She was still far weaker than she was willing to admit, following the blade she took to the gut at the hands of Virgil Bunt, may his soul rot, but exercise would have to wait today. "Julia and I have some things we need to take care of. Ship's business."

Genevieve smiled. "So, she's accepted your offer?"

"You knew?" Julia asked, her eyes narrowing suspiciously at her friends.

Merri snorted. "Oh, honey. Everyone knew."

Branna didn't share their mirth, still apprehensive about the conversation to come. "Gen, if you know where Gus is, would you please send him up to our room with a copy of the ship's Articles, and ask him to bring the item he's been holding onto for me?"

"Of course."

"We'll be taking breakfast upstairs. Can you have something sent up for us?" Branna added.

"I'll take care of that, now."

"Thank you." Branna gave a soft tug on Julia's hand to lead her to the stairs. "Come on. I have some more to tell you about."

Branna entered the room and immediately stripped out of her clothes and washed up, her mind already on all the things they had to go over, ticking off the points in her head that she needed to make. She wondered if Julia had agreed to this too hastily. Her face must have registered her unease.

"What's wrong?" Julia murmured into her neck and slipped her arms around her waist from behind.

Branna didn't answer but let herself relax into the embrace for a moment before straightening and turning out of Julia's grip at the knock on the door. "Get dressed. We'll talk over breakfast."

Julia didn't speak as the serving girls moved around the room while she quickly washed up and changed. She had clearly felt the shift in Branna's mood, and she waited until they were alone again to begin the conversation. "Are you having second thoughts?"

"No. But you may be. Sit and eat something." Branna gestured to the table and waited for Julia to sit before she began again. "I know you've already agreed, but I want you to know that if at any time you change your mind, for any reason, it won't change anything between us."

"I won't. I want to come with you—"

"Just wait and hear me out. Then I'll ask you again after you have all the information. I've already spoken with Genevieve and there's a place for you here at Travers. You'll be challenged and useful and I think you'd really enjoy it."

Julia crossed her arms. "Are you trying to talk me out of this?"

"I just want you to know what your options are."

"I'll keep it in mind."

"Julia, I'm not trying to make this difficult. There's just a lot I need for you to know. I don't want you to feel misled, and in turn resentful if we do this."

Julia's expression softened. "I'm listening."

Branna closed her eyes briefly. Her fifteen-year path of vengeance for the murder of her parents ended in a bloody battle that claimed the lives of seven of her crew—and countless others before that—and severely damaged her ship. As desired, it also led to the death of Captain Cyrus Jagger, his crew, and the sinking of his ship. "I wish I could say what you saw and experienced in the battle with the *Serpent's Mistress* was as bad as it ever gets, but I can't promise that. What we do is dangerous and uncertain all the time. It's also exciting and rewarding, and at times mind-numbingly boring."

"I understand."

"And when we return to sea, I am the captain of the ship first and your lover second."

Julia's eyes narrowed and she opened her mouth to speak.

"What I mean to say is, I have to make decisions every day to ensure we do good work and the crew and ship stay safe. You may not always like what I have to say or the orders I give, but I expect you will respect and follow them as do the other crew."

Julia frowned. "Why would you think I would do otherwise?"

A smile tugged at the corner of Branna's mouth. "Because I know you. You have a sharp mind, sharp temper, and a sharp tongue and are not afraid to use any of them. Especially, when it comes to me. It's part of what I love so much about you. You challenge me constantly. But out there you cannot question me, at least not where others can hear. In private, if you want to lay into me about something, offer a suggestion or idea, then I want to hear about it. I also love your intuition, thoughtfulness, and creativity. It will be invaluable to me, and the rest of the crew and I regard your counsel like no other."

Julia nodded, seemingly mollified at Branna's words. "I won't do anything to threaten or undermine your authority, Branna."

"Yes, you will, but I know it won't be intentional." She reached across the table to take Julia's hand. "This is uncharted water for me too, and I'm not such a fool in love to think that this isn't going to take a lot of work and we aren't going to make mistakes."

Julia gripped Branna's hand. "Except if I make a mistake someone could get hurt."

"I live with that fear every day. We all do. We just do the best we can and do better next time."

Before Julia could speak again there was a knock at the door and Branna rose. "That will be Gus."

Her first mate, Augustus Hawke, had been her savior, mentor, confidant and friend for fifteen years since he found her, the lone survivor of her parents' raided and destroyed merchant ship.

"I brought what you asked." Gus handed Branna a rolled copy of the Articles. "She hasn't changed her mind yet, has she?"

"Not yet, but I'm doing my best." She turned back to see Julia finally picking at some food on her plate. "If she still wants to come after several hours of going over this drivel then I'll know she's serious—or crazy."

"Then she'll fit right in." He handed her a long leather case. "It's really well done, Branna. I think I might be a little jealous."

"Is it? I haven't seen it yet."

"She'll love it. Well, if she's into that kind of thing."

"All right, I must get back. I want senior officers at supper tonight, Merri and Gen, too. Also, ask Ollie, er, Oliver to join us for a drink," she added, referring to her former ship's boy who had grown into a fine young man and valuable member of her crew practically overnight.

"I'll see to it, Captain."

Branna leaned the case against the wall by the door and rejoined Julia at the table. "How are you doing?"

Julia smiled. "I'm still with you."

"Okay." Branna set the Articles on the table. "Before we get to that there's something else."

"You're making me nervous."

Branna held her gaze. "You should be, I think. Your sailing skills and experience are expert, no one is questioning that, and I have no doubt that you are equally skilled in recordkeeping and accounts."

"But?"

"As a member of my crew you will be expected to defend your ship and crewmates in battle."

Julia winced. "I need to learn how to fight."

"Yes. You do."

"I don't know, Bran."

"I don't want this to scare you. And I'm not talking about turning you into a killer, as if that could ever happen. But

I need to know you can protect yourself and others. Do you understand?"

"You'll teach me?"

"No. I have too much training of my own to do right now to get back into shape. I've asked Jack to teach you with a cutlass and basic hand-to-hand fighting skills."

"Why Jack?"

"Because you and he share weaknesses and strengths. He's not big and by extension not as strong as many men we encounter. His advantage comes from his quickness, creativity, and being underestimated, and he is great at close-quarters fighting. He's the best for what you need to learn, and he can teach you fast."

Julia stood, moving from the table to the open balcony overlooking Nassau's bustling harbor. She needed a moment to quiet her chaotic thoughts. She replayed much of what Branna had told her and Bran was right about everything. She would have to be careful to hold her tongue in front of the men. She may have been offered a position of authority with the crew, but Branna was the captain and Julia needed to honor that at all cost, lest she damage Branna's relationship with her crew or their own relationship.

She could do that. She was certainly willing to try. Learning to fight, though, made her stomach clench. She had fought for her life before, but she had never killed. She knew that's not what Branna expected of her and she knew she would fight to protect Branna. She would kill to protect Branna or any of her friends or family if necessary. The crew would be no different.

She turned back to Branna and met her expectant gaze. "When do I start?"

Branna studied her closely. "Are you sure, Julia?"

"Yes. My place is with you. I'm not letting you go either."

"I was hoping you'd say that." She got up from the table and retrieved the case by the door, setting it on the table in front of her. "I had something made for you."

Julia arched a brow in interest and opened the case. Her eyes went wide as she took in the gleaming iron blade of the cutlass. It shimmered as sunlight bounced off the metal of a slightly curved blade just two feet long, and three inches wide. The grip was tightly braided leather around a smooth brass hilt with an elegantly bowed handguard.

She reached out, her fingertips just brushing the weapon, its beauty in stark contrast to the damage she had seen something like it inflict. Next to it was a polished black leather scabbard and belt, she assumed to wear around her waist.

"Do you want to try it on?" Branna asked.

"No." Julia jerked her hand away. "I mean, it's beautiful. I just…it's a lot to take in. I just need a moment." She didn't want to hurt Branna's feelings, but this was all happening so fast. She was afraid she was losing herself already.

"It's all right, Julia," Branna said as if reading her mind. "I don't want you to change and I'm not trying to make you into something you're not. Your gentleness and kind heart, your love and compassion, are what make you the stunning woman I love, and I don't want you to ever lose sight of that. No matter what. I just need to know you can keep yourself safe. I won't always be able to, and I didn't think you would want that. Was I wrong?"

"No," Julia agreed with a small smile. "You're not wrong."

Branna tucked a loose lock of hair behind Julia's ear. "I know this is a lot. Do you want to take a break?"

"No. Let's finish."

Branna moved the case to the floor, and they returned to their places at the table. She unrolled the Articles and scanned the pages. "I usually have to read these to the new crew, but in your case, I think you're capable of going through them at your own pace. Let me know if you have questions."

Julia read through the pages carefully, pausing now and again to ask for clarity, point out a vague or easily misinterpreted area and offer suggestions for change. It was well past midday when she restacked the pages and signed her name to the list of crew. She was exhausted and overwhelmed.

"Are you hungry?" Branna asked. "Do you want me to have something brought up?"

"No, thank you." Julia moved to the bed, stretched out and flung an arm across her face to block out the light to stave off the headache she could feel threatening behind her eyes. "I think I just want to rest for a while."

"Do you want to be alone?"

"No. Please stay."

Branna crawled into bed next to her and slipped her arm around Julia's shoulders, encouraging her to roll over. Julia happily complied and tucked her head into the crook of Branna's arm and shoulder and draped a hand across her chest.

Branna held her, gently kneading loose the tension in Julia's neck and shoulders with one hand while the other skimmed softly along her bare arm. Julia sighed, relaxing farther into her embrace. While she was anxious to get started, a part of her wanted to stay like this forever. She knew once the *Banshee* sailed again, moments like this with Branna would be few and far between.

CHAPTER THREE

Julia sat at the table, lost in her own thoughts, as the conversation and laughter of her friends filled the air around her. Less than a year ago she was running Farrow Company, the largest shipping company in South Carolina. She spent long days keeping records, negotiating new contracts, and occasionally going out on a sail with one of her crews. She'd had only one relationship she would have even counted since Branna left as a young woman and was presumed dead for fifteen years. She had a few friends, but besides her sisters, she had never felt as connected to anyone as she did to this group.

They had been through so much together and she couldn't imagine her life without them. She could barely remember her life before, though she missed her sisters, Alice and Kelly, often. She knew they would be all right. They were alive and safe and had each other.

She felt Branna's eyes on her again. Branna was giving her space but silently checking in on her from time to time. Julia met her gaze and smiled reassuringly. She hadn't changed her mind.

She was excited about their life together and the adventures and challenges it would bring. She just needed time to think and process how everything had changed so drastically for her in such a short amount of time.

Julia saw someone approach over Branna's shoulder and smiled. Oliver walked hesitantly up to them and came around so Branna could see him.

"You asked for me, Captain Kelly?" His voice was deep, that of a man's, and he seemed to grow daily, but he was still all awkward arms and legs in ill-fitting clothes.

Branna stood and extended her hand in greeting to that of a shipmate, not a cabin boy. She pulled out a chair and gestured for him to join the table. "Mr. Swansborough, thank you for joining us."

He sat awkwardly and seemed completely bewildered at being treated as an equal. He fidgeted with his hands and his knee jiggled up and down, giving away his nervousness. "Thank you."

"Swansborough?" Julia questioned, her eyes flicking around the table.

"Yes. The only people who know who Oliver is are at this table," Branna explained. "He is the son of Charles and Abigail Swansborough of Port Royal and heir to their shipping business. We try to keep his family ties quiet so as not to make him a target. He will be taking over the family business one day, but until then, his parents have entrusted him to my care."

Merri snorted into her drink. "Ya done a right swell job with that, by the way. What with leading 'im on a years' long path of vengeance an' bloodshed."

"Merri," Jack Massey, *Banshee*'s quartermaster and Merri's lover, hissed. He shot Branna a nervous look of apology while Merri simply shrugged, daring Branna to come back at her.

"I understand," Julia cut in, attempting to head off a confrontation when she saw Branna's thunderous expression. She smiled at Oliver. "It's a pleasure to formally meet you, Oliver Swansborough. I spent some time in Port Royal with your family. Your parents were very generous and your sister,

Elizabeth, was delightful. I very much enjoyed my time with them."

"Thank you, Miss Farrow." Oliver smiled proudly.

Branna went on, "Now that you're here, Oliver, I can let you know when we take the *Banshee* out at the end of the week, we'll be heading to Port Royal first. It's time for us to reconnect with folks and find out what's going on out there. What news have you had from your family?"

Oliver frowned. "I haven't heard from them in a little while. I usually get letters from my sister every few days. There are so many ships coming back and forth between Nassau and Port Royal it's easy to stay in touch. Not lately, though. I don't know why."

Genevieve straightened in her chair. "That's odd."

Branna eyed her. "What?"

"I haven't heard much from them either. There's never a shortage of talk coming out of Port Royal, but lately everyone has been tight-lipped. When I've asked, I get these vague nonanswers. I have a shipment of goods for the Swansboroughs. They should have sent a ship for them a week ago, but I haven't heard anything. I didn't really think much of it, but now I wonder if something is wrong."

"I guess it's a good thing we're headed that way. What's the cargo?" Branna asked.

"Rum, textiles, lumber, and some other odds and ends," Gen said.

"We'll take it with us." Branna turned back to Oliver. "Was there anything in the last letter from your sister that may be of some help?"

"News of the family, my parents, and cousins that live with us. Oh, my sister did mention a new ship in the area out of Tortuga, the *Ferryman*. Captain Isaac Shaw, I believe. He's had some people on edge with his crew causing problems in town and in the bar. She really didn't go into too much detail."

Branna nodded. "Sounds like we need to introduce ourselves to Captain Shaw."

"Sounds like," Gus agreed with a wry smile.

Conversation quieted for a moment until Oliver piped up again. "My cousin, Bridget, will be pleased to see you, Captain. She's been worried about you and wanted to come to Nassau, but my father wouldn't allow it."

Gus coughed into his drink and Gen glared at him, a thump beneath the table suggested she may have kicked him. Merri grinned at Branna who stared wide-eyed at Oliver, her mouth agape.

"Who's Bridget?" Julia asked, sensing the obvious tension.

No one answered and when she looked around, everyone found something to busy themselves with.

"Jack," Branna blurted, "will you be ready to start working with Julia tomorrow morning?"

"Yes, Captain. Looking forward to it."

Branna turned back to Oliver. "Thank you for joining us, Mr. Swansborough. If you hear from your sister before we sail, please, let me know."

Oliver had been dismissed and rose to leave. "Yes, Captain, I will."

"Who is Bridget?" Julia snapped.

"I think we're done here," Branna said.

Gus and Jack stood so fast to leave their chairs nearly tipped over and they were gone in a mad scramble.

Before Julia could ask for a third time about the woman Branna clearly did not want to talk about, there was a loud crash and angry shouting from the bar that turned all heads in that direction.

"I'm tellin' ya she's out there!" a loud drunk voice shouted.

There was laughter and more shouting jeers from the men taunting the speaker.

"You're drunk, Blythe!"

"And crazy!"

"Go home, ya mad fool!"

"Bugger all," Gen muttered and pushed out of her chair. "Give me a hand?"

"Aye," Branna sighed and together they moved over to the bar.

"Settle down!" Genevieve barked as she moved toward the growing mass of men.

"What's going on?" Julia asked Merri, storing away questions of Bridget until later, while she watched Gen and Branna wade into the crowd.

Merri sipped her drink and rolled her eyes over to the bar. "It's just Thomas Blythe being drunk and raving again. It happens every few months or so."

Julia could hear the shouting and laughter continue and Genevieve's voice trying to defuse the situation. "What's he upset about? Who's out where?"

Merri topped up her drink. "'Bout a year ago a ship went missing. The *Windswept*, apt name, don't ya think? Thomas's brother Alden was the first mate an' Thomas the quartermaster."

"What happened to her?"

"No one knows. She just never came back. She'd only been out a week between 'ere an' Tortuga. There were no storms ta speak of, no attacks that anyone 'eard of, no debris was ever found an' no crew ever turned up. She just vanished."

"What about Thomas? He's here."

"He was injured at the time an' couldn't sail with them."

"Lucky for him."

"Not sure he sees it that way. He lost 'is brother, 'is mates, 'is livelihood."

"Did no one look for her?"

"They did. Ships went out fer weeks, months even. Word was out fer anyone who sighted her ta make contact or take note of their position an' let someone know. She's never been seen. She's gone."

"Thomas Blythe doesn't seem to think so."

"He's never gotten over his brother's disappearance an' he's never stopped looking. When he's not passed out drunk somewhere, that is."

Whatever Julia was going to say next was cut off by the crash of breaking glass and an enraged scream from one of the men at the bar. She turned back in time to see the entire mass of them break out into a brawl, fists and chairs flying, bottles breaking. Julia jumped to her feet. "Bloody hell!"

Merri grabbed her arm. "That'd be ill-advised, hon."

"But Branna and Genevieve—"

"Can take care of themselves."

Branna tried to fight her way to the center of the crowd, clearing a path for Genevieve.

"Everyone needs to calm down or clear out!" Gen shouted.

Branna could barely see over the press of large bodies in front of her. The men continued to shout and shove at each other. She could hear Thomas Blythe raging on about the *Windswept*. Calling men cowards for giving up on her.

She grimaced. This was not going well. She started picking off the stragglers from the outside of the mob. Grabbing them by the collar and throwing them back to thin the crowd. They sometimes straightened looking like they wanted to start swinging until they saw who had relocated them. They slunk away after that. She had made short work of half a dozen or so when she felt the tension rise. She had been doing this work for far too long not to sense real danger.

Branna grabbed Genevieve by the arm as she was pushed and jostled about, and shouted over the din, "You still have that blunderbuss behind the bar?"

"Aye."

"Get it!" Branna shouted just as a man stepped to the center and shoved Thomas Blythe and poured a drink over him. Blythe, already drunk, staggered back and crashed into a table, showering its occupants with booze and that's all it took. The mob erupted in fisticuffs.

Branna pushed her way to the center of the crowd where three men were beating soundly on Blythe with fists and boots. She growled her displeasure at the one-sided fight and threw a punch to the kidney of the first man.

He arched, grabbing at his back, and whirled around. His eyes went wide at Branna's thunderous expression, and he took off through the crowd. The other two hadn't seen her yet and continued to pound Blythe as he lay on the ground, trying to protect his head and chest from the blows.

Branna grabbed the next man, spinning him toward her and breaking his nose with a swift jab to his face. Blood spurted and he shrieked in pain before he staggered from the bar. The last man had picked Blythe off the ground, apparently wanting to get in a few licks with his fist. Branna was shoved from behind into him just as he cocked his arm back and she took his elbow hard to her right eye, snapping her head back, her teeth clicking together jarringly.

Branna grabbed her face with a wince and roared her anger. He turned and she charged him just as a deafening explosion sent everyone ducking and diving for cover.

Genevieve stood on the bar, the muzzle of the blunderbuss smoking and debris raining down on everyone from where she sent the scattershot through the thatched roof of the courtyard. "Everyone out! Now!"

The mob scattered in seconds and within minutes the bar was empty of drunken sailors. Branna helped Thomas Blythe to his feet until she righted a chair and pushed him to sitting. "Okay, Blythe?" she asked.

His lip was split and blood trickled from his nose and mouth. He had a gash above his eye, which was swelling shut. Branna looked around and grabbed a rag from the bar and a near-full ale that, miraculously, hadn't been overturned. She set them both in front of him.

"Branna," Julia called when she and Merri hurried over to them as soon as it was clear. "Are you all right?"

"Yes, I'm fine."

Julia winced and touched Branna's face. "Ouch."

Branna touched her swelling eye. "It's nothing."

Genevieve arranged bonuses for whatever kitchen and serving crew got the bar put back to rights before the end of the night. She grabbed a bottle of rum and a handful of glasses. "Come on, let's move back to the courtyard and get out of their way."

Branna helped Thomas Blythe to his feet, leading him back to their table. Julia joined them after collecting a bowl of warm water and some rags.

Julia sat in front of Blythe and waited for him to drink down the glass Genevieve set in front of him. "Mr. Blythe, we haven't met. I'm Julia Farrow. I'm going to clean up your face and it may sting a bit."

"I know who ya are," he slurred and winced as she dabbed the cloth at the cut over his eye.

Genevieve's mouth was set in a hard line. She was not pleased. "You want to tell me what that was about, Thomas?"

His eyes darkened, glittering with anger. "She's out there. She has ta be."

"The *Windswept*?" Genevieve asked and Thomas nodded slowly.

"What makes you so sure?" Branna asked, humoring him.

His eyes glittered. "I can feel it in my bones. She's out there."

Branna shook her head. "It's just not possible. Someone would have seen her. She would have headed to port for help. There's no way."

He slammed his hand on the table, making everyone jump and overturning the bowl of now blood-tinged water. "She's out there!"

"Looks like someone got beat with the jackarse stick," Merri muttered.

"I ain't no fool!" Blythe rocketed out of his chair and pointed a finger around to them all and then pinned Branna with a hard, angry glare. "And yer a fuckin' selfish coward just like the rest of them."

Branna stiffened, clenching her hands in anger at his challenge as he staggered out of the courtyard.

"Never mind him, Branna," Gen said. "He's drunk and doesn't know what he's saying."

Julia toyed with her glass. "You don't believe him? That the ship could still be out there?"

Branna was silent for a long time. "I wish I did. I just don't see how it's possible."

"Well, that's enough nonsense fer me fer one night." Merriam stood and finished her drink before turning toward her room.

Genevieve nodded. "I better go supervise the cleanup efforts. Do you two need anything?"

"No, thank you," Julia replied.

Branna sat, brooding, and poured herself more rum. She shook her head to Genevieve's question.

Julia moved around the table and sat next to Branna, placing a hand on her arm. "What he said just now really bothered you?"

"No, I'm fine."

She couldn't explain why she felt so stung by his accusation of cowardice. At the time the *Windswept* went missing, she was consumed with hunting down and destroying the *Serpent's Mistress*. She had kept a look out for the ship, but she had never aided in the search. She wasn't willing to deviate from her mission, to lose Jagger's trail. Maybe if she hadn't been so single-minded, she would have been able to do something more to help.

"Branna?" Julia persisted.

"I'm going to bed. Are you coming?"

"Of course." Julia stood and laced her fingers with Branna's as they climbed the stairs together.

CHAPTER FOUR

Branna stood in front of the open balcony doors, watching the starlight glinting off the rippling water as Julia moved around the room making herself ready for bed. She could feel Julia's questions hanging in the air, but it seemed she wasn't going to ask. She had questions herself—how had so much of her past reared its ugly head in a matter of minutes? She didn't even know where to start making sense of what she was feeling about everything that had happened tonight. Perhaps, talking it out with Julia would help. It usually did. "You can ask me about her," she said finally.

"I don't need to, Branna." Julia sat down on the bed. "We've had this conversation before. It's not my business. I don't need to hear about all your meaningless relationships."

"She wasn't meaningless."

"Oh."

"Bridget Bennett and her three younger siblings, a boy and two girls, came to live with the Swansboroughs after their parents died of illness. I spent a lot of time in Port Royal chasing down Jagger and the *Serpent's Mistress* and we became…close."

"Did you love her?"

"Yes, but not the way you mean. You saw what I was like just a few months ago. Five years ago, right after the *Banshee* launched, I was even more angry and obsessed. Bridget was a comfort. She's sweet and safe and I cared about her very much, as much as I could care about anything but my own vengeance, I suppose."

"What happened? Why didn't it work?"

Branna sensed no jealousy from her. Only compassion and genuine interest in what her life was like. "It wasn't right and we both knew it. She wanted me to change. She needed me to give up the sea and be safe for her and that was something I couldn't be. I don't think I could ever be."

"You never wanted to try again?"

Branna crossed the room to kneel in front of her, her hands on Julia's knees. "Never. It's only you, Julia. It's always only been you. What we have, the way you make me feel, I can't even explain. If you asked me, I would give up the *Banshee* in a heartbeat."

"I would never ask that of you, Bran. It's who you are."

"I know. And that makes all the difference. You've given up so much for me. Tell me what I can give you in return."

"You can tell me about Thomas Blythe and what about the *Windswept*'s disappearance haunts you so."

Branna wasn't ready to talk about that. She had made peace with her past with Bridget Bennett. Not so with her failure to help find that ship. "Another time, I will."

Julia caressed Branna's cheek. "In that case, you've already given me everything I need. A sword and scabbard to hang it in."

Branna blinked at her for a moment before throwing her head back in laughter. She pushed Julia back onto the bed and straddled her, pinning her arms to the bed. "It's a cutlass, you ninny."

Julia laughed with her and wriggled her hips. "A cutlass then. What more could a woman want?"

Branna leaned over her, her gaze lingering on the rise and fall of Julia's chest, her breasts straining against the thin material of her night shift. "I can think of something you might enjoy."

Julia licked her lips, obviously aware of what Branna had in mind. "I think that might be a purely selfish gift on your part."

Branna released Julia's hands which immediately tangled into her hair. "You don't even know what it is yet," Branna teased as she trailed kisses down Julia's neck and across the swell of her breasts.

Julia was still half off the bed which made what Branna intended all the easier. She moved her hands over Julia's body through the thin material, her belly tightening at Julia's moan of pleasure as she slid back to her knees and slowly smoothed her hands up Julia's legs, lifting her shift.

She kissed up along the inside of one thigh while tracing slow patterns across the skin of the other. Julia's breath came out fast and harsh and the scent of Julia's arousal had Branna's head spinning.

Branna worked her way back up, pushing Julia's legs apart before closing her mouth around her center and parting her with her tongue.

"Bloody hell, Bran." Julia gasped and flung an arm across her face with a groan of pleasure.

Julia's cry sent a flash of heat between Branna's legs and drove her to suck and nip at Julia with wild abandon.

Julia bucked, her legs clenching against Branna's head so tightly she feared her neck might snap. She teased Julia with sharp quick flicks of her tongue before sucking her fully into her mouth again.

"Oh, my God."

Branna worked to hold on to Julia as her hips rocked wildly against her mouth. The beginnings of her own climax stirred deep within her. Branna had never come solely from pleasuring someone else and was trembling, her belly clenched tight with the feeling. She knew when she sent Julia over the edge she was bound to go, too.

"Don't stop."

Branna quickened her pace again, sucking Julia into her mouth, laving her with her tongue. Julia jerked and went still for a moment before her body shuddered violently and erupted in an orgasm that had her screaming Branna's name.

Branna slipped a hand from Julia's hip, sliding it between her own legs and pressing hard against her center as she, too, tipped over the edge.

Julia groaned and collapsed back onto the bed, her eyes hooded and glassy. Branna sat back on her heels gulping a breath and wiping Julia's arousal from her face with her hand.

After another moment she pushed herself to her feet and gathered Julia into her arms, helping to pull her more fully onto the bed.

"You came, too, didn't you?" Julia murmured.

"Aye," Branna said and nipped at Julia's lower lip.

"Totally selfish."

"How does that feel?" Branna asked and tightened the belt another notch.

"It feels a little awkward," Julia admitted.

Branna stood back and considered how the belt and scabbard hung at Julia's left hip so she could draw the cutlass with her right hand. "You'll get used to it."

"That's what I'm afraid of."

"Julia, if you're having second thoughts—"

"No. No, I'm sorry. It's just going to take me some time." She looked down at herself in pants, shirt, and boots, now with a wide leather belt around her waist and the scabbard and cutlass swinging at her side. "I think I look ridiculous."

"You don't." Branna gave her an appraising glance. "Trust me."

"Is that so?" She draped her left hand over the hilt of the weapon and affected an exaggerated imitation of Branna's walk as she swaggered across the room, her still much-shorter hair bobbing up and down. She spun and came back the other way laughing at Branna's aghast expression. "Because it's occurred to me that this all may be some ploy to act out some twisted fantasy on your part."

Branna scowled. "Tell me that's not how you think I walk?"

Julia stopped, her hands on her hips. "Just kiss me."

Branna slipped her hands around Julia's waist, pressing their bodies together and brushing her lips across Julia's in a teasing kiss.

"More," Julia murmured and snaked her hands around the back of Branna's neck.

Branna obliged and deepened their kiss until she heard Julia sigh deeply.

"Are you staying to watch?" Julia asked.

Branna pulled away and slung her own scabbard and sword across her back. "I can't. I'm going out to the ship to go over it with Gus and Nat. I don't even know about all the upgrades yet. We're running some stationary rigging drills and I need to go aloft and loosen up. It won't go well for me if my body gives out a hundred feet up. In the afternoon we'll be sparring on deck, so I probably won't see you until supper or after."

"I understand." She pulled Branna in for another quick kiss before they headed downstairs to meet Jack. Branna gave him a wave before heading on to the repair yard.

It was well past supper by the time Branna returned to the courtyard and found Jack and Genevieve chatting over a bottle of rum. She dropped into a chair at the table and reached for a glass and the bottle. She took a long drink and wiped a dribble of rum from her chin.

"How did it go?"

"Much better than I thought it would, actually," Jack said. "She's good. Quick and instinctive. Her endurance needs work, but this is only day one and she's never moved like this before. She works hard, has good focus and a good attitude. I think she's going to be quite skilled in time."

Branna was unsurprised by Jack's assessment. She couldn't imagine Julia not being good at whatever she turned her mind to. "How far can you get her in the time we have?"

"If we can devote the time we have left here, push hard and get some time on deck before we hit Port Royal, I'd say she'll have a decent command of the basics."

"Will I have to worry about her?"

"Under what circumstances would you not worry about that woman?" Genevieve asked dryly.

Branna waved her off. "You know what I mean."

"She'll be able to handle herself," Jack said. "I'll see to it."

Branna glanced around. "Where is she?"

"We worked hard today. I believe she's gone up already," Jack replied.

"Did she eat?"

"I saw to it," Genevieve said. "Worried already?"

"Enough out of you. I'll see you both in the morning?"

Genevieve raised her glass in salute and Jack nodded.

Branna pushed open the door quietly and had to shove hard against an obstruction on the floor. She slipped in through the narrow space and saw Julia's clothes and boots in a pile in front of the door. The cutlass in its scabbard was leaning carefully against the wall.

The moonlight through the room was enough to see Julia asleep on her stomach and naked but for the sheet carelessly draped across her waist and legs. Her fair skin shone in the half-light and Branna's heart did a little flip at the sight of her.

She stripped out of her clothes and washed as quickly and quietly as she could manage, but Julia didn't stir at all. Branna slipped into bed next to her, leaning over her to brush the hair from her face so she could kiss her cheek softly.

Julia stirred but didn't fully wake. "Hi."

"Are you okay?" Branna asked as she smoothed a hand over Julia's bare back.

"Sore." Julia sighed at Branna's touch.

Branna kneaded the muscles of her neck, shoulders and back, eliciting a groan from her. "Too much?"

Julia shook her head. "It's nice."

Branna worked out the knots she found one at a time, smoothing the muscles back into place. After only a few minutes she could tell Julia had fallen back asleep. She didn't stop the massage, as she knew Julia would feel better for it in the morning.

It was going to be a busy week for all of them, getting the ship and her crew ready to sail again. But ready they would be.

CHAPTER FIVE

Present Day

Julia absently rubbed a hand over her arm, bruised where Thomas Blythe had grabbed her, as she stood on the deck of the *Banshee* while Nassau grew smaller and smaller. She promised herself she would make the time to discuss his situation again with Branna—tell her what happened—and see if there was anything they could do to help him, but now was not the time. She pushed thoughts of him and their upsetting confrontation on the dock out of her head.

Her new leather boots creaked when she shifted her weight to rest her left hand across the hilt of her cutlass, slung low on her hip. Even after only a week, it was a stance so natural now she was barely aware of it.

Her hair was loose and whipped around her head as the *Banshee* came up to full sail and surged away from port while the sun rose higher. Despite what had happened on the dock earlier, she felt light and giddy, excitement building within her at the thought of her new life as crew of the *Banshee* and partner to Captain Branna Kelly.

A flush of warmth crept up the back of her neck and she turned to see Branna watching her from the quarterdeck with sharp, glittering eyes. Julia smiled at her, and Branna visibly struggled to keep from grinning back at her like a fool.

Julia wasn't on duty now but had much to do before Port Royal. Branna had set up a strict schedule for her and she wanted to make her proud. Training with Jack in the morning, crewing the noon-to-four watch and the evenings spent working on the accounts.

She had already peeked into her office and seen the ragged stack of ledgers and receipts she had to go through and groaned inwardly at the thought. As much as she'd love to stay and enjoy more of the day, she had to get to work.

* * *

Four days into their sail to Port Royal and Branna couldn't be more pleased. The refitted ship was a dream and the crew, running rigging drills on each shift, day and night, was working together nearly seamlessly. The seven new crewmen were inexperienced, but Branna had taken a risk and put the least experienced of them on watch with Julia. She was an excellent sailor and had a way about her that let her instruct them without embarrassing them or damaging their confidence. Only a few times did Julia have to put one or two in their place for getting a little too handsy with her, and if it hadn't been so much fun to see, Branna might have been furious.

As she suspected, she and Julia had little time to spend together because of their respective duties. They managed to steal a few moments of intimacy as they passed through her cabin, and they held each other close on the nights they were able to share the bed, but beyond that they hadn't been together since they left port. They were only a day out of Port Royal now and Branna had every intention of putting their lack of togetherness to rights.

She stretched, her back cracking and her gut pulling with an ache that she feared would never heal completely after nearly dying from a knife wound less than three months ago. She was more than ready to turn the wheel over to Gus at the change of watch. The night sky was brilliant as the ship cut through the inky waters toward Port Royal. With a nod to Gus, she ducked down into the galley to retrieve the tray of food she had asked be prepared for her and Julia and headed off to her quarters to find her. She hadn't seen Julia since her watch ended and she hoped she wouldn't have to wake her. But if she did, she knew just how she was going to do it.

Branna frowned when she pushed open the door to her cabin. The lantern was lit low, but the room was empty. She set the tray on her desk and moved quietly across the floor, easing her way through the narrow doorway to Julia's quarters. Julia was hunched over her desk, her hair piled messily atop her head and pinned in place with a pencil. There were piles of paper scattered everywhere and she flipped a page of the ledger she was currently going through as she twirled an errant lock of hair around her fingers.

"Hi," Branna greeted.

Julia's head jerked up and her hand flew to her chest as she sucked in a breath. "You startled me."

"I'm sorry." Branna frowned at the lines of fatigue around Julia's eyes. "You're working too hard."

Julia gestured to the mess on her desk. "Have you seen this disaster? It's a wonder you all have any money to do anything at all."

Branna feigned hurt. "I thought we were doing a pretty good job."

"Well, it looks like everything is accounted for, but between you, Gus, Jack, Nat, and whoever else you had scribbling transactions, you've managed to make all this virtually impossible to decipher."

"That's why I hired the best."

Julia didn't even notice as she searched for something on her desk, lifting the book and shuffling pages, scattering some onto the floor. "Damn it. Have you seen my pencil?"

Branna plucked the pencil free, letting Julia's hair fall away loosely. "Julia, you don't have to get through all this in one sitting. There's plenty of time."

Julia scrubbed her hands over her face. "What time is it?"

"The watch just changed." Branna picked up the fallen pages.

"It's eight o'clock already? God, did I miss supper?"

"Julia, it's midnight."

Julia stared at her. "No, it's not."

"Come on." Branna held out her hand.

"I just need to finish one thing."

Branna huffed impatiently when Julia opened the ledger again. She retreated out the door and slipped out of her shirt. "Come to bed, Julia," she called and stuck her arm back through the doorway where she knew Julia could see it and waved her shirt in the air before dropping it on the floor.

Julia laughed and the ledger closed with a thump, hopefully for the rest of the night.

"I need something to eat," Julia called from her office.

"Music to my ears," Branna said, picking up the tray.

"Food, Bran. I need food." Julia's eyes went wide when she crossed into the main cabin and saw her, topless but for a strategically placed food-laden tray.

"Ask and you shall receive. And then maybe you can tell me what you'd like for dessert?" Branna made no effort to hide her desire.

Julia grinned and took the tray from her, letting her gaze rake shamelessly over Branna's body.

She had finally gained the weight back following her injury and had gotten a great deal stronger, though still not where she had been before she had been stabbed. Nothing aroused Branna more than the way Julia looked at her. "I'll just be over here." Branna crossed to the bed, stretching out with her hands tucked behind her head, a smile pulling at the corners of her mouth. "When you're ready."

"Maybe I'll just save this for later?" Julia set the tray back on the desk before slipping into bed next to Branna and running a hand across her chest.

Branna's arms wrapped around her tightly. "Why, Miss Farrow. I thought you'd never ask."

Branna's eyes snapped open a split second before there was a sharp rap on the cabin door.

"Speak," she called, her voice gravelly with sleep.

"You're needed on deck, Captain," Gus said from the other side of the door.

"What is it?" Branna untangled herself from Julia.

"A ship sighted ahead. It may be adrift or in distress."

"How far?" Branna sat on the edge of the bed and scrubbed her face as Julia stirred next to her. A quick glance at the gray sky out the window told her it was just dawn. They had only been asleep for a few hours.

"A few hours at this speed."

Branna nodded, though Gus couldn't see her. "I'll be there shortly."

"Aye, Captain."

Branna washed quickly and pulled on clean clothes, being as quiet as possible.

"What is it?" Julia asked sleepily.

Branna sat on the edge of the bed and looked at her. Her face was creased from the bedding and there were dark circles under her eyes. "I don't know yet. A ship in distress maybe."

"Okay." Julia threw the sheet off and made to rise.

"No." Branna put a hand on her shoulder. "Stay here. There'll be nothing to see for a while."

"But I should—"

"You're not on duty. Get some rest, and for the love of God eat something." Branna gestured to the tray of food that had gone untouched.

Julia sighed. "Is that an order, Captain?"

"Please," she said and brushed her lips across Julia's.

Julia smiled and dropped back onto the bed. "Your wish is my command, Captain."

Branna kissed her again. "I'll see you later."

Branna strode across the deck and climbed to the forecastle to join Gus, and Nat Hooper, her giant deep-voiced bosun. "Mr. Hawke, report."

Gus handed her the spyglass. "We saw a light a couple of hours ago. A fire. We thought a ship was aflame, but it never changed in size."

"A controlled signal fire on deck, perhaps," Nat said.

Branna held the instrument to her eye and sighted the ship. It was a small two-masted schooner. Less than half the size of the *Banshee*. The ship bobbed gently in the water but was still too far away to make out much more than that. Branna could see no fire and no movement on deck. "What do you think?"

Gus shrugged. "Could be an ambush. It's an old tactic. Feign distress and take over the ship that comes to your aid."

Nat grunted. "If they try that on us that would make them the stupidest men at sea. We're more than twice their size."

"Indeed," Branna considered. "They could be in trouble, too. Hold course and let's find out."

"Aye, Captain." Gus moved off to return to the wheel.

Branna turned to Nat. "Assemble a boarding party and have them stand by."

The sun grew higher, and Branna could clearly see the ship without aid. She could also see a cluster of men on deck waving their arms. Perhaps they were what they seemed. "Reef the sails," she called, and the men scrambled to take in the sails and slow the ship. "Come along the starboard side and throw the boarding hooks."

She caught movement below as Julia emerged from the cabin. She was armed and Branna raised an eyebrow in question. "Expecting trouble, Miss Farrow?"

Julia looked up at her, mouth quirked in half a smile. "Always, Captain."

Branna dropped down from the quarterdeck and came to stand at the gunwale with Julia and watch as her crew skillfully maneuvered the *Banshee* alongside the smaller vessel. She got her first look at the captain and his crew.

"Good morning, Captain," she called across the few remaining yards as her crew threw lines across and the other men caught them and tied them off. "What seems to be the trouble?"

The man grinned, showing a mouth full of rotten teeth. "Ran over a loose net, I think, and it's fouled our rudder."

Branna flinched inwardly at his unkempt appearance but kept her face blank. "Why not send someone down to cut it loose?"

The man's smile faltered briefly and he looked embarrassed. "I'm afraid we don't have any swimmers here. If I could just speak with your captain a moment perhaps, we can work out a trade for your services."

Branna bristled but maintained her composure, though she was unable to hide her disbelief at their predicament. It appeared they *were* the stupidest men at sea. Only a fool went out with no one who could swim. "I see."

"Can you help us out, miss? I would be very grateful."

Though they were all armed with some form of blade they didn't seem a threat and she was inclined to lend a hand. "Mr. Hooper, please see if the twins are available and willing to assist Captain…" She trailed off and eyed the man.

"Moore, miss. Captain Robert Moore."

The brothers, Eli and Albert, were not actually twins and had come to the crew from the repair docks. Their sailing skills still needed polish, but they could fix anything and had already proved themselves invaluable. Nat didn't have to go far to find them as most of the crew was hovering on deck to watch the events unfold.

Branna turned back to Captain Moore. "Permission to come aboard, Captain Moore?"

His face darkened briefly before the smile returned. "Is that necessary, miss? Can you not just send the men down from your ship?"

Branna's eyes narrowed and she felt Julia stiffen beside her. She had been willing to believe they were harmless until that very moment. They had something to hide and now Branna was determined to find out what.

She returned his smile. "It will be safer for my men to go in the water from your ship if they get a better idea of what kind of damage has been done first. If that doesn't suit you, Captain, we can take note of your position and send someone back for you when we reach Port Royal?"

He frowned and looked at his men who waited tensely to see what he would do. "Fine. Fine. Come over," he snapped.

Branna turned and nodded to Nat. He had eight men standing by. She would go too, and as she made ready to climb the gunwale Julia gripped her arm.

"I'd like to come," she said.

Branna's first instinct was to say no but she stopped herself. She wasn't sure what was going on, but she was confident if trouble broke out, they could easily overpower this crew. She didn't want to start out this sail by holding Julia back.

"Very well." Branna nodded and was about to reach her hand down to help her when Julia jumped up on the gunwale and swung across with the rest of the men. Branna gave a small shake of her head and followed her across.

She dropped onto the deck of the smaller ship, her crew a little behind her and Nat and Julia to her right. She extended her hand. "Captain Moore, I'm Captain Kelly of the *Banshee*."

The man's eyes widened in recognition and surprise. He knew who she was and he wasn't expecting her. If this was a trap it hadn't been for her and she hoped, now knowing who she was, he thought better of it. She didn't bother introducing anyone else. They weren't going to be here long.

Captain Moore finally collected himself and shook her hand. "Thank you for your help, Captain Kelly."

"Well, let's see if we can provide that help." She jerked her head at the crew. "Let's take a look."

CHAPTER SIX

The *Banshee* crew along with Moore's crew moved back to the stern to check the damage. Julia stayed where she was and surveyed the deck. It was in ill repair, the lines snarled and sails frayed at the ends. The deck was buckling in places and crates were stacked haphazardly along the gunwales. Smugglers, maybe. She eyed the crates and saw a flash of movement out of the corner of her eye. Probably rats.

She turned back to the line of men bent over the stern, gesturing and talking about the best way to free the rudder. Branna stood with her arms crossed a little back from them and kept them all in sight. To someone who didn't know her she appeared relaxed, but Julia could tell she was hypervigilant and would remain so until they were off this ship. The *Banshee*, powerful and intimidating, bobbed a few meters away with Gus on the quarterdeck watching everything.

Despite the relative safety of the situation Julia felt her unease build. Something was very wrong here. Something moved again between the crates and this time she pinned the creature with her eyes. Down near the deck between two rotten crates were wide, frightened eyes peering back at her from a filthy, dirt-streaked face.

Julia's mouth parted in a small gasp at the shocking sight of the child—a girl—and she looked terrified. Julia took a step closer, and the girl flinched and shook her head sharply, lank, greasy hair tumbling into her eyes. Julia's heart thudded but she understood. The girl didn't want Julia to give her away. She strained to see through the shadows. There were bruises on the girl's face and blood on her lip. She had been mistreated recently.

Anger welled up in Julia. She knew that kind of fear. She gestured with her hand to tell the girl to stay there and stay quiet and the girl nodded in understanding.

Julia moved over to Branna, keeping her voice low. "There's a child here. I believe she's captive."

Branna tensed but otherwise didn't acknowledge the information. She turned to Gus on the *Banshee* and gave him a sharp nod of her head. A signal he would understand. "Mr. Hooper?" she called conversationally and waited for him to turn to her, the rest of the men still engrossed in the conversation and the twins just beginning to strip to go in the water. He met her gaze, and they exchanged the same unspoken signal.

"Secure the ship!" Branna commanded, drawing her sword, and the deck exploded into chaos.

The *Banshee* crew drew on Moore and his men who were more than happy for a fight. Blades clashed as the men, all clustered together, fought and cursed for space to attack and defend.

"I want them alive," Branna shouted.

Julia stepped forward, a hand at the hilt of her cutlass and Branna jerked her back.

"No. Stay here. That's an order," Branna added before stepping into the fray and slashing at the nearest man.

Julia gritted her teeth and stepped back. The fighting was ugly, furious and loud and would be over soon. Moore's men were wild and untrained. One of them was already dead, his blood pooling onto the deck.

Branna took on two men, one of them Moore, when a shriek of terror behind Julia drew her attention. There was another man coming up from belowdecks, dragging a girl who cried and kicked and bit at his hand. It wasn't the same girl she'd seen. That girl was jumping around the man's feet screaming at him to stop and hitting him with a broken crate slat as he moved toward the port side.

Julia chanced a quick glance back at the fight. It was waning but the men were all still engaged. She turned back just as the man backhanded the girl with the crate shard, sending her flying across the deck. Julia was horrified as he picked up the smaller girl and made to throw her over the side.

"No!" Julia drew her cutlass as she charged him.

He threw the crying girl over and whirled at Julia's scream. He wasn't expecting her and just reached for his weapon when she slammed into him, driving her blade up under his ribs, piercing his heart. Warm, thick blood fountained over her hands, the metallic scent powerful this close. She released the hilt and he dropped to the deck.

She didn't spare him another glance as she looked over the side and could barely see the girl floundering in the swells. She'd already drifted away a good distance. Julia never took her eyes off her as she kicked out of her boots, unbuckled her scabbard and climbed the gunwale.

She dropped in feet first, trying to keep her head above water and the girl in her sight. She could see only a small mop of blond hair floating on the surface and swam powerfully toward her. The water wasn't cold, but she didn't want to be in it for long. She surged through the swells, stopping every few strokes to make sure she still knew where the girl was. She could see her, but it was taking forever to get to her. Distances were so disorienting in the open ocean.

Branna turned when she heard Julia scream and saw her charge after the man with the struggling girl. "Julia, no!" Branna yelled but couldn't turn her attention from Moore for too long. He wasn't the complete idiot his men were.

She battered him back for a few minutes longer until the rest of her crew descended on him, disarming him and forcing him to his knees. His remaining crewmen were dead or disarmed.

Branna sheathed her sword and ran for the side, sparing a quick glance at the dead man, Julia's cutlass jutting gruesomely from his chest. Panic clawed at her chest until she spotted Julia between the swells, the girl tucked under her arm as she side-stroked back to the ship. She was still a ways out, but by the time Branna lowered the boat, Julia would be back at the hull. She needed to find another way to get them back up.

She searched the deck, finding nothing but frayed lines and trash.

"Here." Nat hoisted a rolled rope ladder, running with it to the side. He tied off the end to the gunwale and threw it over, the ladder unrolling to the water line.

Julia had reached the ship with the girl. She reached for a rung of the ladder and held on tightly with one hand and to the girl with the other but appeared exhausted and could do no more.

Branna could see she was struggling and her jaw clenched. Branna wanted to be the one to help but she wouldn't be able to bring Julia and the girl up on her own. "Nat!"

"I'll get her." He swung down the ladder.

Branna held her breath while Nat climbed down to them. She couldn't hear well, but true to form, Julia refused help until the girl was safe.

Nat dragged the girl from Julia's arms, and she hung limply as he slung her over his shoulder and climbed up as far as the waiting arms of the crew, who lifted her carefully to the deck.

He descended the ladder again and pulled Julia up and swung out around her, reaching a hand around her waist to help her up the rest of the way.

Branna's heart was in her throat as Nat helped Julia over the side. Branna eased her to the deck when it was clear she was too shaky to stand on her own. "You're okay," Branna said, more for her own benefit then Julia's. "You're okay."

Julia smiled at Branna and was assaulted by two small bodies as the girls flung their arms around her neck and sobbed unintelligibly. Julia returned their embrace from where she was seated and whispered soothing words. Her gaze drifted to the body of the man she had just killed, and she swallowed heavily, looking away.

Branna frowned. She wanted to get Julia back to the *Banshee*, get her dry and make sure she was all right. Her own words came back to haunt her. Captain first, Julia's lover second. She gritted her teeth and turned to her crew. "Mr. Hooper. Secure this ship. Go through it top to bottom. If there is a brig or a hold here, lock these men up. If not, lock them on the *Banshee*."

"Aye aye, Captain," he replied and started issuing orders to the crew.

Branna shouted to be heard aboard the *Banshee*, "Mr. Massey, please help Miss Farrow and the girls back to the ship and see to their health."

"Aye aye, Captain," Jack replied and swung over to the ship.

Branna watched as Julia, the girls clinging tightly to her, made her way, with Jack's help, back to the ship. She longed to follow. Captain first, she repeated to herself.

It was hours again before Branna felt like the ship and their charges were under control. Nat and a crew of six men would sail Moore's vessel back to Port Royal, Moore and the crew secured in the hold for the trip. It had taken some time to get the net from the rudder and the ship ready to make the trip. She wasn't in good shape and Branna was looking forward to turning them over to Charles Swansborough.

They would be slower now so the ships could stay together. If they pushed through the night, they could be in Port Royal tomorrow evening. Throughout the afternoon Branna's emotions vacillated between anger at Julia for behaving so recklessly, anger at herself for not protecting her, and immense admiration at her courage in saving the children.

"Captain?" Jack said.

"Mr. Massey. How are the girls?"

"Frightened and hungry. They've been beaten, though it's nothing that won't heal. They've had a rough time of it, but they should be all right. They're resting now."

"Good. And Julia?"

"Shaken, mostly. Nothing that food and rest can't fix."

"Where is she?"

"Back in your cabin."

"Thank you, Jack."

"Captain, she did well today. I saw the whole thing and if not for her, those little girls would surely have been killed."

"Did you tell her that?"

"I did. But I think she may need to hear it a few more times. She's having a hard time with what happened. With what she had to do."

"I understand." She hoped she hadn't made a mistake bringing Julia here. Maybe this wasn't the place for her. She had wanted to come but nothing Branna could tell her would really prepare her for what it was really like to fight. To kill.

Julia had killed before—Cuddy Hurst—but Branna had protected her from that because she didn't want her to have to live with that knowledge. Branna couldn't protect her anymore and she had just thrust her in a dangerous situation and Julia had reacted the only way she could.

Branna's guilt must have shown all over her face as she hesitated, kicking at the boards of the deck.

"She doesn't blame you, Captain," Jack said.

"What?"

"It's not your fault what happened."

Branna was unconvinced. "Let me know when the girls wake up. We'll need to speak with them when they're ready."

"Aye, Captain."

Branna pushed open the door to her quarters. She thought, perhaps, Julia would be resting. She should have been anyway. She wasn't in the cabin and Branna crossed to her office. Julia sat behind her desk, flipping through the ledger again. There was a bottle of rum nearby and a glass in her hand from which she sipped.

"What are you doing?"

"I never got a chance to finish going through the entries from the repairs. I need to get back to it before I lose my concentration." She drained her glass and moved to refill it, her hand shaking so much the bottle clinked against the glass rim.

"Julia, you shouldn't be doing this now."

"Why not?" she snapped and drank down her glass again, grimacing as the liquor burned her throat. She reached for the bottle again. "I'm fine."

Branna stopped her with a hand on her wrist. "No, you're not. You're shaking."

Julia swallowed heavily and looked at her hands as they trembled in front of her. "It's nothing. It's nothing."

Branna gripped Julia's hands in her own. "It's okay. You're okay."

Julia couldn't meet Branna's gaze. The tremors moved from her hands up her arms until her entire body shuddered and she lurched to her feet, pushing past Branna toward the open window astern. She lunged for the rail and vomited over the side.

Branna was right behind her, gathering her hair from her face and rubbing soothing circles across her back. "Breathe, Julia. It's okay."

Julia retched for another moment before dropping to her knees, tears spilling down her cheeks. "Oh, God." She sobbed as she clutched her middle and rocked to comfort herself. "Oh, my, God."

Branna's heart broke for her. She didn't want this for her. This was so selfish. Killing someone, no matter how justified, stole a piece of your soul every time and she had just expected Julia to give that up for her. And Julia had without a second thought. She had done everything Branna had asked of her and more, and Branna, in turn, had taken her hand and everything she offered so freely and walked her right into this.

Branna gathered her into her arms and rocked with her. "I'm so sorry, machree. I didn't mean for this to happen."

Julia buried her face in Branna's chest and clutched at her shirt as gut-wrenching sobs wracked her body.

Branna held her until she quieted, smoothing a hand across her back. "Julia, what you did was incredibly brave. You did what you had to do to save the lives of those little girls. Everyone knows that."

Julia finally pulled away and met Branna's eyes. "I know. In my head, I know. But my heart hurts for what happened."

"I understand. It will take some time and the pain of it never goes away completely but it will get better." She brushed tears from Julia's face with her thumb. "I promise."

There was a soft knock at the door. Branna helped Julia to her feet and waited a moment for Julia to straighten her clothes and finger comb her hair. "Come," she said.

Jack entered. "I'm sorry to bother you, Captain. The girls are awake, Julia. They're pretty upset, and I think you should come."

"Thank you, Jack. I'll be right there."

Jack backed out of the room and Branna turned to her. "Julia, you don't have to—"

"I do. I want to."

Julia had pulled herself back together but the tension around her eyes gave away her grief. Branna extended her hand. "We'll go together."

Branna followed Julia into the infirmary, the former purser's cabin. It had been redone with two bunks and storage beneath. The girls sat huddled together on one of them. Clean now, they looked even younger than before, and the bruises stood out starkly against their pale skin and frightened eyes.

Julia sat on the bunk with them, and they both clutched at her desperately. She hugged them tightly to her. "You're safe now. No one is going to hurt you. Can you tell me your names?"

The older girl straightened and said clearly, "I'm Anna and this is my sister Lillian."

"Bennett?" Branna blurted. "Anna and Lilly Bennett?"

The girls looked at her wide-eyed and the older one nodded.

Branna hadn't recognized them. She hadn't seen them in some time. She crouched down in front of the bunk. "Do you remember me? I'm Branna, your sister Bridget's friend."

Julia gasped and Jack grunted in surprise.

Anna nodded, tears filling her eyes. "Branna."

"That's right. You know your cousin Oliver is here."

Lilly's eyes brightened and she asked in a small voice, "Ollie?"

"I'll get him," Jack said.

A minute later Oliver burst into the room. "Oh, Jesus! I didn't recognize them when they came aboard." He crossed the room and Julia moved out of the way as the girls hurled themselves at him, wrapping their small arms around his neck and crying and talking at once.

Their words were a jumble through their tears, but Anna kept crying, "He's dead, Ollie, he's dead."

Oliver pulled away to look at them both. "Who, Anna? Who's dead?"

Tears spilled down both their cheeks. "Uncle Charlie," Lilly wailed, identifying him the way she knew him and not as Oliver's father.

Oliver made a strangled sound. "What?"

Branna and Jack shared a look of horror and Julia's hand flew to her mouth.

Anna tried to explain in a hysterical little-girl way. "They said it was an accident at the docks but no one believes it. He killed him. He killed Uncle Charlie."

Branna placed a hand on Oliver's shoulder. His face was red with disbelief, grief, and anger, but he managed to remain composed. "Who killed him, Anna?" he asked.

"Captain Shaw," she said, her voice suddenly low and eerily menacing for such a young girl.

"Anna," Branna said, "where's your Aunt Abigail and cousin Elizabeth? Are they all right?"

Anna nodded. "Aunt Abigail took sick with grief. She was at the house and Elizabeth was seeing to her. Jeremy, too," she added referring to her older brother.

"How long ago did this happen?" Branna asked.

Anna looked at her sister. "I don't know. I don't know how long we were..." Her voice got small and trailed off.

"It's okay," Julia said. "Don't worry about that. You're safe now."

Branna looked at the two girls. She couldn't believe she hadn't recognized them. They looked so much like Bridget. "And your sister? Is she all right?"

Anna's face darkened. "I don't know. She had been working at the bar. Captain Shaw asked her to sit with him a lot. She was scared all the time."

Branna's jaw clenched in anger at the description. The girls maybe didn't understand what they were saying but Branna did. Her gaze flicked to Julia who looked both angry and frightened.

"We were on our way to see her. But we never got there. Those men..." Anna trailed off and began to cry again.

Oliver stood up suddenly, his face a mask of rage and pain. "Captain, we must—"

"Stand easy, Mr. Swansborough," Branna said. "I understand how you feel. We will take care of this."

CHAPTER SEVEN

The *Banshee*, with Moore's ship behind, sailed into Port Royal at dusk the next evening. Branna stood on the quarterdeck with Gus at the wheel. Two ships, not much bigger than Moore's, stood sentinel on either side of the harbor but made no move or act of aggression.

As they sailed farther in, she saw a magnificent ship that rivaled the *Banshee* in size. She looked well outfitted and from the way she sat low in the water, she was heavy with guns. Branna knew in her gut that this was the *Ferryman* and her chest tightened with apprehension. She didn't want to have to face that ship in battle.

She remained vigilant. The *Banshee*'s cannon ports weren't open, but the gun deck was manned and ready if there was trouble. Her crew stood on the deck, armed and tense as they drifted to a stop and dropped anchor.

"Lower the boat!" Branna called and motioned for Gus to join her in her cabin. "Mr. Massey, you're with me," she yelled across the deck and Jack scrambled to join them.

Julia was finishing getting dressed. She looked better rested, but there was still a haunted look to her that had Branna worried. She just needed to give her time. Over the last day, and with Oliver's constant attention, the girls had begun to recover their spirit and acted more like the children they were. She hoped there would be no long-term damage from what they had endured.

Branna turned to Gus. "We're going ashore. I need to find out what's going on. Jack, I want you to take Oliver and the twins. Escort the girls home to the Swansborough house and stay there. Make sure everyone is okay and find out as much as you can about what is going on here and what happened to Charles Swansborough. We will come to the house tomorrow."

"Aye aye, Captain," Jack replied and stepped out to round up the men.

"Gus, retrieve Captain Moore only. He's coming with us. Make sure he is secure. I want him seen when we head to Swans Tavern. Tell Nat to keep his crew on board the ship and keep watch. The rest of the men are to stay on the *Banshee*."

"What are you going to do?" he asked.

"I'm going to the Tavern. I have a feeling that's where I'll find this Captain Shaw and I would like to introduce myself."

"What about me?" Julia asked.

"You're coming with me." Branna wasn't sure what the safest course of action was where Julia was concerned, but she didn't want to let her out of her sight. Julia was uncannily perceptive, and Branna wanted to use that. She would see things from a perspective Branna couldn't.

Gus nodded. "Aye, Captain." He disappeared out the door to collect his charge and pass along the orders to Nat.

Branna glanced at Julia. She was in pants, shirt, and boots and Branna stopped her as she moved to buckle on her scabbard and cutlass, which Nat had cleaned and returned to her.

"No," Branna said, and Julia looked up, confused. "I want you to change. Wear something nice. No weapons."

"What? Why?"

"I don't want them to see you as a threat. I want them to underestimate you."

Julia scowled. "You mean you want me to distract them."

"Call it whatever you like. If you go in there armed, they'll be wary of you and if trouble starts, you'll be a target."

"If trouble starts, I won't be able to defend myself," Julia argued.

"You won't have to."

"Because you'll fight them all and protect me?"

"No, because we'll get out of there." Branna gripped Julia's arms. "Please, just trust me."

Julia held her gaze for a long moment before unbuttoning her shirt.

When they arrived at the dock, Jack, Oliver, and the twins surrounded the girls, and they moved quickly off toward the Swansborough's estate. Gus made a show of shoving the bound and gagged Captain Moore along the dock while Branna and Julia followed behind. Branna armed herself to the teeth while Julia wore a simple skirt and blouse with only a dagger slipped into her boot.

They were met with open stares of surprise, hostility, and apprehension as they moved along the path to Swans Tavern, the Swansborough Company's establishment. Branna paused in the entrance, motioning for Gus to wait with Moore by the door. She surveyed the room. It was packed and reeked of smoke, liquor, and unwashed bodies. The laughter and conversation were loud, but where she remembered this place to be one of relative safety and good humor, she now felt a menacing air about it.

The men looked hard, and their eyes glittered in the low light as they turned to watch her walk across the room, Julia close by her side and casting a wary glance around. Branna didn't know who she was looking for, but she had a feeling Captain Shaw would make himself known.

She was halfway across the room when a flash of brown hair caught her eye. Bridget was here. She was serving a tray of drinks to a particularly rowdy table and Branna bristled when she saw one of the men grab Bridget from behind.

Julia put a restraining hand on Branna's arm, and she forced herself to relax. This wasn't the time, and she breathed a sigh of relief when Bridget managed to extricate herself from his grasp without too much trouble.

Bridget turned then and saw Branna, her eyes going wide in surprise before a torrent of emotions flickered across her face—relief, fear, and confusion.

Branna waited as Bridget crossed the room, her anger rising as she took in her unkempt appearance, hollow cheeks and an ugly bruise around her eye.

"Branna," Bridget hissed. "What are you doing here?"

Branna ignored the question and cupped Bridget's chin to tilt her head, getting a better look at her face. "Who did this to you, Bridget?"

Bridget flinched away from her hand, her gaze flicking to Julia. "You shouldn't be here, Branna." Her eyes scanned the room, and she looked back over her shoulder at someone Branna couldn't see. "Please, I don't want any trouble."

"With respect, Miss Bennett," Julia said, "it seems you already have trouble."

Bridget looked at her again more closely, her gaze flicking back and forth between them and understanding dawning as she took in the way they stood near each other, Branna partially shielding Julia from the room.

"Aye, that I do. But *you* don't. Not yet," Bridget said and checked behind her again.

Branna stepped closer to her and lowered her voice. "Your sisters are safe, Bridget. They're with me. They're safe."

Bridget gasped and her shoulders sagged with relief as tears filled her eyes. Before she could speak, a large hand clamped down on her shoulder from behind and she jolted straight.

"Aren't you going to introduce me to your friends, my pet?" the man asked. His voice was deep with a hint of island accent suggesting he had lived here for a long while. His head was shaved and skin bronze from the sun, but his eyes were light, so not likely a native. His smile flashed impossibly white teeth as he stared hard at Branna.

Bridget opened and closed her mouth a couple of times but couldn't seem to find words, apparently, still reeling from the knowledge her sisters were out of danger.

The meaty hand moved from Bridget's shoulder and extended to Branna. He towered over her and seemed to enjoy using his size to intimidate. "Captain Isaac Shaw."

Branna held his gaze and took his offered hand. "Captain Branna Kelly."

His eyes brightened with recognition, and he appraised her again, his gaze falling on the black jade pendant around her neck. "The Raven. I'm delighted to meet you. I heard about your troubles, Captain Kelly. I'm pleased to see you've recovered."

"As am I," Branna agreed.

His attention turned to Julia and his eyes glittered with unabashed desire as he looked her up and down. "My dear." He reached for Julia's hand, and she allowed him to take it and press the back of her hand to his lips. "Captain Shaw, at your service."

"Julia Farrow," she said calmly enough, though Branna knew from the wary look in her eyes she was feeling anything but. "It's a pleasure to meet you, Captain."

"I assure you, Miss Farrow, the pleasure is all mine." He looked her over again and frowned. "Farrow. Of the Farrow Company's *Firelight?*"

Julia tensed, looking like she wanted to crawl out of her skin. Just like Branna rarely spoke of the destruction of her parents' ship, she didn't often speak of the loss of her crew and her time captive aboard her own ship with her dying men. "Yes."

"I'm sorry for your loss," he said, and Branna almost believed him. "I understand you were the only survivor."

Julia was rigid and looked as if she might shatter with her next breath. "That's right."

"I'm so very glad that you did," he said sincerely before turning his attention back to Branna. "I met Cyrus Jagger a few times."

"Oh?"

"He was an arsehole."

Branna nearly laughed. "I couldn't agree more. And what would Jagger's opinion of you have been?"

"I'm sure he thought I was as charming and agreeable as everyone else does. So, Captain, what brings you to my port?"

"*Your* port? I am looking for Charles Swansborough. I need to turn over some men we caught a day's sail from here. Kidnappers and abusers of children." She turned and stared pointedly at Gus and Moore by the door.

She turned back around in time to see Captain Shaw staring hard at Moore, his eyes narrowed. It was clear he knew Moore and was not pleased he had been apprehended.

Shaw's mouth turned down. "I'm sorry to have to tell you, Captain. Mr. Swansborough met with an unfortunate accident at the docks a week ago. He did not survive, I'm afraid. I have agreed to act in his stead as master of this fine port."

"I'm very sorry to hear that," Branna said, her gaze flicking to Bridget who was staring at the floor and rocking from foot to foot.

"As his acting agent I would be happy to take the offenders off your hands." Shaw raised a hand over his head, and in a moment a man, even bigger and darker than Nat Hooper, came to stand at his side. "My first mate. Everyone just calls him Angus."

The man nodded a greeting.

"Angus will be happy to accompany your man to collect Captain Moore, his ship and his crew," Captain Shaw said.

Branna took advantage of his slip at the use of the name she hadn't provided. "You know him?"

Captain Shaw's eyes darkened momentarily, but he never lost his composure. "Only by reputation."

Branna cocked an eyebrow at him. "Of course."

Angus stalked off across the room, motioning to a couple of men as he went. They converged on Gus and spoke a few words. Gus looked to Branna and she nodded her agreement. She would turn the men over, though she knew, if Shaw let them live, they would be back on the water within days. She didn't have enough information yet and now was not the time for conflict. She watched as the men disappeared out the door.

"Now that the unpleasantness has been handled allow me to buy you a drink, Captain. Miss Farrow?" Shaw offered the crook of his elbow to her.

Julia flashed Branna a pained glance but took his arm, letting him escort her to his table. He held a chair for her, and she smoothed her skirt beneath her and allowed him to seat her with a huge hand at the small of her back. Branna took a chair next to her.

"Bridget," he barked. "Drinks for my new friends."

Bridget flinched and hurried off to fulfill his request, returning in a moment with clean glasses and a fresh bottle of rum.

"Now, Captain," he said, his eyes bright with interest. "You must tell me about your battle with the *Serpent's Mistress*."

CHAPTER EIGHT

The air in the captain's quarters was solemn, the silence filled with worry and apprehension about what they had seen and heard. Julia moved around the room quietly setting glasses in front of Nat, Gus, and Branna as they sat around Branna's desk. She filled them up with rum and poured one for herself. There was an empty chair for her, but she took her drink and folded herself onto the bed, tucking her legs under her.

They had spent the better part of the evening drinking with Captain Shaw and a few of his men. Julia could still feel their eyes on her, and she shuddered inwardly. Branna had shared with them the story of the *Serpent's Mistress*, and though she told the truth of it, somehow Julia felt betrayed at hearing her most painful memories shared and laughed about with a company of men no better than Captain Jagger himself. Hearing it out loud, seeing the men's eyes shine with excitement at the most violent and terrifying moments, made her sick to her stomach.

She knew Branna didn't do any of that to hurt her, but she needed space from her to catch her breath. She felt vulnerable and the only thing she could think to do was sit apart from her.

"I'm not looking forward to crossing blades with Shaw's man, Angus," Nat said to break the silence before tossing down his drink.

"Christ, I know." Gus slid the bottle to him. "He's one big bastard."

Branna took a sip from her glass and looked to Gus and Nat. "I don't think we'll ever be able to prove it, but I believe Captain Shaw did kill or have killed Charles Swansborough. I assume, so he could take over the port. Hopefully, his family will be able to fill in more about what's been going on and how this all started."

"He seems entrenched here and from what I could tell, he has money and support," Gus added. "It's going to be hard to get him to leave."

"I wonder what happened to Swansborough's associates?" Nat asked. "I guess they all cleared out."

"Or were killed," Gus said.

"I don't think so," Branna said. "We would have heard if ships or people started disappearing. Captain Shaw seems to be working hard at making people believe he's benevolent despite the violence surrounding his rise to power. He seems to think of himself as a real charmer, a real ladies' man."

Gus scoffed. "Bugger that. I saw Bridget's face."

Branna's expression darkened and she tossed back her drink. "I let him know about the cargo we have for the Swansboroughs. He's been gracious enough to take it off our hands. For below market value I might add."

"Genevieve will not approve," Nat commented.

"Yes, well, it gives us a legitimate reason to stay in port for a few days to unload and I want it off the ship. If we need to move fast, we're not going to want the extra weight."

The conversation quickly ended after that. There was nothing more to say until they had more information. Branna walked Nat and Gus out and shut the door, leaning her head against the wood for a moment. "Julia, you haven't said a word since we came back. Please, tell me what's on your mind."

Julia finished her drink before unfolding herself from the bed. She didn't want to talk. She doubted she could sleep. "I think I'm going to get some work done before morning."

"Now?" Branna stopped her as she made for her office. "Julia, please, tell me what's wrong."

Julia stopped. She wasn't being fair. None of this was Branna's fault and shutting her out wasn't going to fix anything. Julia had wanted this. She had asked for it and gone into this with her eyes open. If anything, Branna had tried to talk her out of it.

She turned around and leaned her back against the door. "I'm sorry, Branna. I don't know what's wrong with me."

"Please, come sit down." Branna pulled her by the hand and guided her back to the bed.

"I just feel so raw ever since..." She dropped her head into her hands. She needed to say it out loud. She needed to name it or it would never get better. "...ever since I killed that man."

Branna knelt in front of her but didn't interrupt.

"And then listening to you tell Captain Shaw about the battle with the *Serpent's Mistress*, hearing him ask questions so detached and void of emotion, it just felt like salt in an open wound." Julia shuddered and wrapped her arms around herself, suddenly chilled.

"I'm sorry. I know that was hard for you. It was hard for me, too."

Julia looked at her now, seeing Branna's concern for her etched on her face. "I understood what you were doing. You needed to find common ground with him. Establish a rapport. I know that. I'm just scared, I think."

Apparently, that was all Branna needed to hear. Her eyes narrowed. "Okay. You're going to go back."

"What?"

Branna rose and paced the room. "I've been thinking I'm going to get the Swansboroughs off the island. They're not safe here. You'll go back with them to Nassau, help get them settled and explain to Genevieve what's going on."

Julia jumped to feet and stopped Branna's pacing with a hand on her arm. "No, Branna. That's not what I'm saying. I don't want to go back. Anyone with a brain in their head would be scared. These are dangerous men. I just feel a little out of control right now. Like things are happening all around me, and to me, and I'm just letting myself get buffeted about."

"What do you want to do, then?"

"I want to help these people."

Branna nodded. "And we will. Together."

Julia had been to the Swansborough family home before. It looked different now, darker, sadder. The pall of grief hung heavily over the house and everyone in it. Elizabeth Swansborough sat across from them with Oliver and Jeremy Bennett, their cousin. She told them their mother, Abigail, was too unwell to meet with them, but she would pass along their condolences on the death of her husband.

"How long has Captain Shaw been in the area?" Branna asked.

Elizabeth was pale and her face creased with worry. "About a month, I guess. He seemed harmless enough at first. He threw a lot of money around, flashed his charming smile and made friends quickly. He started undercutting the prices for goods. We think he was threatening the other merchants to bow out of negotiations. My father caught wise to what he was doing early on and threatened him with sanctions. The wrong thing to do, I guess. Shortly after that my father was crushed by some toppling crates down on the docks."

Julia's heart ached for the vibrant woman she had laughed with less than a year ago. So much had changed for her in such a short time—so much tragedy. Julia understood what she was going through and would do whatever she could to help. "Did your father normally supervise loading and unloading of shipments?"

"No. Never. He had been called down to mediate some dispute. I have no idea what. We believe it was a ploy to get him there."

Branna shook her head. "I can't tell you how sorry I am about all this, Elizabeth."

Elizabeth's eyes shone with tears, and she pressed her lips together to fight them off. Oliver wrapped an arm around her shoulders. "Are you going to help us, Captain?" he asked.

"Yes, but first, I want to get you and your family off the island. There must be merchants still loyal to your family who can help. It's not safe for you here."

Elizabeth cleared her throat and wiped her eyes. "Thank you, Branna, but we've already tried. It may look like we are free to move about, but I can assure you this house is being watched. Captain Shaw will already know you're here. We've tried to leave. He smiled and told us he needed us here in the event he had any questions or needed our counsel regarding the company. The threat was clear, however."

"There must be somewhere you can go," Julia said.

"We can go to the farm," Oliver suggested.

"What farm?" Branna asked.

"We have a sugar plantation," he said. "It's well staffed and remote. We would be safer there. I don't think Captain Shaw will spare the men to come after us. They don't know the land like we do."

"Do it," Branna said. "All of you get out there as soon as possible. Oliver, you'll see to it. Take the twins for added support, but I need Jack with me. We need to get out of here. If Shaw is watching the house, we need him to believe we only came to pay our respects. We can't stay too long."

"Aye, Captain." Oliver stood. "I'll make sure they're safe."

"I know you will, Mr. Swansborough." Branna offered him a small smile. "Elizabeth, what about Bridget? Does she still live here? She should go with you, too."

"No. She has someone she lives with in town. Bridget's been, I don't know, marked by Captain Shaw. Even without holding her sisters' safety over her head, I don't know if she can get away from him. I don't think he'll let her go."

Branna's eyes darkened, her voice low and dangerous. "He will. I'll see to it."

"Who is she living with?" Julia asked. "How do we find her?"

"Mary. She keeps the books for the company. I don't know what's become of her since Captain Shaw showed up, but as far as I know she's around and okay. Ask someone at the bar and they should be able to tell you where to find her."

Branna nodded and turned to go. "Thank you, Elizabeth. Stay safe."

Elizabeth stopped her with a hand on her arm. "Whatever happens we appreciate everything you've done for us." Her gaze flicked to Julia and a ghost of a smile played across her lips. "I'm pleased you two found each other. Please, be careful."

They hustled back through the streets, Branna stalking ahead. Julia didn't need to be a mind reader to know what she was thinking. They needed to get Captain Shaw out of Port Royal. She wished it would be as easy as simply sinking his ship, but he had too many friends and if they were all like Moore, they would have to be cleverer than that.

They were almost back to the docks when a blur of motion streaked toward them. Branna drew a knife, rounded on the person and slammed them against the wall. A small woman, with dark hair and wide frightened eyes, peered at her from beneath the hood of her cloak as Branna pressed her blade to her throat.

"Captain Kelly?" the woman gasped.

"Who wants to know?"

Her voice trembled. "You must help her. I think something terrible has happened. She didn't come home last night, and no one has seen or heard from her."

"Branna, easy." Julia placed a hand on Branna's arm and moved the knife from the woman's throat. "Mary?"

She nodded. "Bridget told me if anything were to happen to her, to find you. That you could help." Her frightened gaze darted between them.

"It's okay," Julia said. "We can help. Tell us what happened."

Mary sucked in a steadying breath. "Captain Shaw has had his hooks in her, but she's always come home. Always. I think he's done something to Bridget. Please, you must help her. I can't lose her."

Branna stepped back and sheathed her knife. "We'll find her."

Julia gripped the woman's hand. "It will be okay."

Mary nodded, tears tracking down her face as she adjusted the hood back around her head and slipped off down the lane.

They sat around Branna's desk again, this time Julia with them. The bottle of rum passed around.

"This changes everything," Gus said. "If he has Bridget and she's alive, he has leverage. He must know we would never sacrifice an innocent life."

"I know," Branna muttered.

"We need to know where she is," Nat added.

"Does Captain Shaw know about your relationship to Bridget Bennett?" Julia asked.

"I don't know. But his taking her suggests so," Branna said.

"She has to be on his ship," Jack said. "Where else would he take her that would be secure?"

Branna drummed her fingers on the table. "We need to know for sure. We need to get on his ship."

Gus snorted. "Oh, sure. Just ask to go look around?"

"We need an invitation," Nat said.

"We need to have something he wants," Jack added. "A Trojan horse."

"What could we possibly have that he wants?" Gus downed his drink.

Julia's heart pounded. She already knew the answer. She closed her eyes for a moment before she spoke. "I know something he wants."

CHAPTER NINE

"Are you out of your bloody mind?" Branna roared, causing the men to flinch.

Julia held up a hand. "Just hear me out."

"No. It will never happen."

"Branna—"

"I said, no!" Her hand slammed down on the table.

Julia opened her mouth to speak again, and Branna shot her a warning glare.

Julia's mouth clicked shut on her words and she pushed away from the table and moved to the balcony doors.

Branna was seething as she looked at Gus, Nat, and Jack in turn. They all looked to each other expectantly. Nat and Jack finally stared hard at Gus.

Gus sighed, resigned. "Captain, it's a good—"

"Out!" Branna screamed and launched herself out of her chair. "Get out!" She knew he was going to tell her it was a good idea, and she didn't want to hear it. The three men scrambled over each other to get out the door.

When they were alone, Branna stalked back and forth across the cabin, her fingers tangled in her hair. Her heart hammered in her chest as she worked to control her breathing. She couldn't remember the last time she was so enraged, though likely it also had something to do with Julia.

She finally stopped pacing and stared at Julia's back. She was stiff with tension and anger. Branna counted out five measured breaths before she spoke. "Say what you're thinking, Julia."

Julia didn't turn around. "You already know what I'm thinking."

Branna started pacing again. "You think I don't trust you. That I don't believe in you and your ability to do this."

Julia remained silent but Branna could hear her working to calm her breathing, probably before she said something they would both regret.

"Tell me, Julia, why would you want to put yourself in that position again?"

Julia did turn now. "I'm not sure *want* is how I would choose to describe it."

"You know what I mean. You've been there before. What Jagger did to you…" She couldn't even think about the condition she had found Julia in, what she had gone through, and Julia didn't talk about it. "Why would you make yourself vulnerable to that again?"

"I'm not, Branna. When I was held on my ship, I didn't have a choice. I was helpless. I'm not now. A woman is in trouble and I can help. I choose this. I'm in control."

"Until you're not, Julia."

"I must do this, Branna. There's no other way."

"We'll find one," Branna pleaded, though she already knew she'd lost this argument.

"She's your friend, Branna. Are you going to tell me my life is worth more than hers?"

"If anything happens to you."

"It won't. I'll be careful."

"Julia—"

"I trust you with my life, Bran. You need to trust *me* with it, too."

Julia was as determined as she was right. They could make it work. Captain Shaw had made no secret of his desire for her. He was no fool and they would have to be clever and careful, but Julia could get on that ship and find Bridget.

"Aye, I do. Let's work it out." Branna threw open the door. "I know you're out there. Get back in here."

Jack, Nat, and Gus materialized from the shadows outside her door and returned to the table.

"He's never going to believe you just defected," Gus said.

"You're right," Julia agreed. "But people believe what they want to believe. He sees himself as charming and charismatic. His ego is enormous, and I can guarantee he would love to win one over Captain Kelly."

Branna sat sullenly at the table and listened to Julia's plan.

"Branna and I have a quarrel in the bar. Everyone sees. He thinks we're at odds, and he has a chance. He's not the kind of man to be interested in women who just throw themselves at him, though I'm sure he's had his share. He needs a challenge. He needs to win, to dominate."

Branna tensed at Julia's description, but she knew it to be accurate. After only spending a couple of hours with the man, she knew he was driven by his own self-importance, his own sense of entitlement.

"When?" Nat asked.

"Why wait?" Julia said. "Tonight."

Julia and Branna walked to the bar arm in arm. Branna was dressed in black leather pants and black shirt. She had left her sword on the ship, but her row of throwing knives gleamed against the black around her waist.

Julia looked down at herself. For all the time and effort she spent training, so far she had spent an awful lot of time in a skirt and blouse, unarmed. This was how she could help. Let him underestimate her and then take advantage.

They entered the bar and found an empty table. As usual the place was crowded and Branna squeezed Julia's hand tightly as they walked by Captain Shaw, holding court with some of his men, with a woman on either side. Julia took note of Gus and Nat as they entered and found space at the bar.

Captain Shaw watched them walk in and Branna nodded a greeting on the way by. He flashed her a toothy smile and appraised Julia openly.

Branna gripped Julia's hand across the table as a serving girl poured them both drinks. "I've changed my mind, Julia. I don't want to do this."

Julia smiled reassuringly. "I love you."

"Let's just go. Let's get out of here."

Julia jerked her hand out of Branna's grasp. "It's too late for that, Branna."

"No. No it's not, Julia. We can leave. We can think of something else."

"Why did you bring me here, Branna? I want the truth."

"What?"

"Remember? To be your partner in all ways?"

"Julia, what are you—"

"What you meant to say was, to keep your books and look good on your arm," Julia snapped, her voice loud enough now that conversations around them were stopping.

Branna was stunned. "What? No. That's not—"

"You demand I respect you and your position, Captain, and in return you'll keep me tucked away so you can dress me up and parade me around in front of your friends like I'm your newest treasure."

Branna's mouth opened and closed wordlessly; her expression devastated to the point it was clear she had forgotten the plan. "Julia, please."

Julia pushed her chair back and jerked Branna's ring from her finger. She threw it onto the table. "Thanks for the ride, Captain. I think this is where I get off."

Branna lunged for her and grabbed her arm. "Julia, wait."

She jerked her arm free and spun, her hand cracking across Branna's face like a pistol shot. Branna never saw it coming and it snapped her head back.

Julia was as surprised as Branna looked and almost took a step toward her when she saw the blood on her lip and the red mark on her cheek. She stopped herself and squared her shoulders. "Don't you dare touch me."

She kept her eyes forward, but it was impossible to miss the glittering eyes and flashing grin of Captain Shaw as she walked by. The trap had been set.

Julia paced their quarters. It had been hours. She stalked back and forth a few more times before the door banged open and Branna wobbled in.

"You're still here? Thought you'd be halfway back to Nassau by now. Did you need help packing?" she muttered.

Julia gaped at her as Branna sat heavily on the edge of the bed and fumbled with her boots. "Are you drunk?"

"Well, I had to make it look good, right? It would have seemed odd if I hadn't been at least a little distraught after your performance."

"Branna—"

"That was a performance, right, Julia?"

Julia winced at her swollen lip and the dusky bruise on her cheek and reached for her. "I'm so sorry I hurt you."

Branna gripped Julia's hand hard before she could touch her. "That's not what hurts, Julia."

"No, Branna, no. I didn't mean what I said. We had to make it look real."

"No one is that good an actor, Julia."

Julia stood abruptly and turned away. She knew she hadn't meant what she said, but was there an element of truth to it? Of course, there was. Her anger was real. "Oh, Branna, I'm sorry."

"Is that what you think? That I'm using you? That you're just some kind of accessory for me?"

Julia could only shake her head, tears burning in her eyes.

"That's not an answer."

"You're right, Branna, this is hard. Harder than I knew and I feel like I'm losing myself. You are so incredible. You have this powerful energy about you all the time and a life and history here that, however painful, enriches you. You know when you got stabbed by Virgil Bunt I knew it?"

"What does that mean?"

"I was at home asleep—safe with my family—and I woke up in a panic with this pain." Julia wrapped an arm around her middle. "Even from hundreds of miles away and half dead you have this pull on me that I can't ignore. And now here I am, and I got everything I asked for and I didn't realize what I'd be giving up."

Maybe this wasn't the time or the place, but she didn't know when was and she needed to get it all out. It wasn't fair to Branna, otherwise. "I had a life, Branna. And it wasn't flashy or exciting and I didn't have a larger-than-life reputation, but it was mine. I built it and tended it and made it comfortable. And before you say anything, I'm not sorry I gave it up. I don't regret coming here or you or anything, so please, stop looking so sad. I'm not leaving you. I just need to find a way to carve out something for myself in your wake. Everything I have here is attached to you. People know me as either the woman who survived an attack by the *Serpent's Mistress* or the woman on Captain Kelly's arm."

Branna was quiet for a long time. "How can I help?"

"That's just it, Branna. I don't think you can. Not with this. I don't know what the answer is, but I do know I have to figure it out on my own or it will just be one more thing that binds me to you."

"You have to know, Julia, I respect you more than anything."

Julia joined her on the bed, sitting close enough their hips touched. "I know you do. I'm sorry for the things I said. I'm so sorry I hit you. I just...Please forgive me. What can I do?"

"Get on Captain Shaw's ship and find Bridget."

"What?"

"It worked. He's more than interested in you, and given another opportunity, I'm sure he'll make his intentions known.

You have intrigued him, and you were right, he sees you as a challenge, a challenge he thinks I'm not up to."

"I am a challenge. You already knew that," Julia said and unbuttoned her blouse. It had been a hard night for them both. She stepped out of her skirt and let it pool around her feet. "Just like I know you are more than up to it."

CHAPTER TEN

While Branna dressed, her gaze frequently traveled to the bed where Julia still slept, peaceful and beautiful. Their lovemaking had been both urgent and tender, passionate and patient, desperate and hopeful.

Julia had reassured her, time and again—with her mouth and hands—their love was strong. Branna had worshipped Julia in kind, and they had fallen asleep in a tangle of sweaty, trembling limbs.

"You're going to make me blush, Captain, if you keep looking at me like that," Julia murmured with a sleepy smile.

Branna tore her gaze from the curve of Julia's hip. "I'm sorry."

"No, you're not." Julia stretched her arms above her head, letting the sheet fall away from her and treating Branna to a generous view of her breasts.

"Christ, woman." Branna covered her eyes with her hand and peeked through her fingers. "Don't do that."

"My apologies, Captain," she teased. "I know how much trouble you have controlling your salacious impulses."

Branna sat at the side of the bed and brushed her fingers across Julia's breasts, and Julia gasped and arched under her hand. "Yes, but control them I must."

"You're a cruel woman." Julia sat up and pulled the sheet to cover herself. "Where are you going?"

Branna slung her sword across her back. "I'm meeting with Captain Shaw today to discuss our sale of the cargo."

"Will we have supper later?"

Branna had an idea to move forward with the plan, but it was best if Julia didn't know the details. "Aye, I'll meet you at the bar."

"Meet me?"

"We're on the outs, remember? We shouldn't be seen together."

"How should I dress?"

"It's your plan, Julia. Make it work."

As anxious as she was about their plan—or lack thereof—to take down Captain Shaw, Julia was pleased to have the day to herself. She spent the morning sparring with Jack and Nat. It was good to stretch her muscles and she was delighted Jack felt her ready to work with two opponents. They moved at half speed, but it was a challenge for her and she loved working through the strategic possibilities.

The afternoon she spent working on the accounts, and as she fell deeper into the work, the hours sped by. When she looked up at the waning light, she knew she had let the day get away from her. She would have to hurry if she was going to be on time to meet Branna.

She smoothed a hand down the front of her dress. It was crimson with a low-cut bodice and elegant black stitching over the full skirt. Merriam had talked her into buying it as a surprise for Branna. She was irritated that this was the occasion Branna would first see her in it, but she had a job to do, and this dress would get Captain Shaw's attention.

She stepped into her boots. She had shoes to go with the dress, but she needed better mobility and also a place to hide a weapon. She slipped the dagger into her boot before running a hand through her loose hair, shaking it out to curl just below her ears.

Jack and Nat were waiting for her on deck to escort her as far as the tavern entrance, after which they would make themselves scarce and keep an eye on things from outside. Gus and Branna should already be there. The men were engrossed in some conversation when Julia emerged. "I'm ready."

The two men turned, their jaws dropping in similar expressions of awe when they saw her. "Whoa," Jack whispered.

Nat recovered first and elbowed Jack in the ribs and he scrambled over the ladder and into the waiting boat below. Nat bowed and offered his hand. "Miss, you look radiant."

"Thank you, Mr. Hooper." She took his hand and let him help her over the gunwale.

Julia wound her way through the crowded bar, scanning the people as she went. She didn't see Branna anywhere. Perhaps she misunderstood where they were to meet. She could feel eyes on her from every corner of the room and she grew increasingly confused and worried.

Captain Shaw appeared in front of her and gave her a low bow. "Miss Farrow, you look ravishing. May I buy you a drink?"

"It's kind of you to offer, Captain Shaw, but Captain Kelly promised me a proper meal to make up for last night's"—she cleared her throat—"disappointment."

"Pardon my saying so, Miss Farrow, but your captain is a first-class fool." His gaze turned toward the bar. "And a liar. She appears to have no intention of keeping that promise."

Julia followed his gaze in time to see Branna and Gus shoot a glass of rum and chase it with a large tankard of ale. Branna slammed the tankard down and, with a laugh, wiped her face with the back of her arm.

Julia's mouth dropped open. Branna was a genius. She had stood her up. "I believe I'll take that drink now, Captain Shaw."

With a jerk of his head the other occupants of his usual table scattered, and he held a chair for Julia and poured her a glass of his finest rum. "You deserve better, Miss Farrow."

Julia sipped her drink and eyed him across the table. She had to be very careful now. She didn't want to make it too easy for him. He had to feel he had won her. "Captain Kelly has been good to me."

He raised an eyebrow. "Forgive me, but that's not how it seemed last night."

"Yes, well, our relationship is not without its difficulties."

"If I may be so bold, I would like to make you a counteroffer."

Julia raised her eyebrows over her glass.

He leaned across the table and took her hand in his. His eyes flashed with excitement and the pulse jumped in his neck. "Sail with *me*, Miss Farrow. Kelly promised to make you a partner. *I* can make you a queen. You say you need respect? I say a woman like you should be worshipped. Choose me and I will give you the world."

"I was under the impression you are involved with the woman from the other night. Bridget Bennett, I believe her name is."

He sneered. "That ungrateful wench doesn't know a good thing when she has it. I will not be keeping company with her for much longer."

Julia breathed an inward sigh of relief. Bridget was still alive. "And how should I interpret that, Captain Shaw? That you are so easily disappointed in your women and cast them aside at a whim?"

He laughed. "I'm not a capricious man, Miss Farrow, I assure you, but you must forgive me my dalliances. With you, though, I see a future."

"That's a generous offer, Captain, but I don't know you, your crew or your ship. I would be a fool to believe you could keep such grandiose promises. And I assure *you*, I am no fool."

He smiled. "Then allow me to show you?"

"Show me what, exactly?"

"My ship, of course. I'll prove to you I am the man I say."

Julia ran a finger around the rim of her glass. "You'll assure my safety, Captain? I believe your crew may not all be as honorable as you."

"I promise you, Miss Farrow, I will be the perfect gentlemen and no harm will come to you." He stood and extended his hand.

"And you'll return me to my ship?"

"Just say the word." His eyes brightened in victory.

"You win, Captain Shaw." She took his hand and let him pull her to her feet. "Let's see this ship you speak so highly of."

The strain of the last few hours was taking its toll. The concentration it took for Julia to maintain a witty, playful conversation with Captain Shaw, while simultaneously looking for signs of Bridget were fatiguing her fast, and a vicious headache hammered behind her eyes. More than once in the last half hour she had to ask him to repeat himself as her mind drifted.

He was thorough which made her job easier. He was determined to show her every inch of the ship and it was massive—larger than the *Banshee*. There were some places she couldn't go of course, and he didn't open every cabin and closet, but she saw no sign of Bridget or any woman for that matter. She was beginning to wonder if this was all for naught.

He beamed. "So, Miss Farrow, what do you think?"

Julia let her gaze roam up and down his body. "I think you and your ship are most impressive, Captain. You have much to be proud of."

Captain Shaw puffed up visibly from her praise. "Thank you, Miss Farrow. I'm pleased you think so."

Julia sighed dramatically. "I've had a lovely evening, Captain, but I'm afraid it's late and I must be returning to my ship."

"But I haven't yet shown you the captain's quarters."

"Thank you, but—"

"Please, Miss Farrow. I am a man of my word, and my intentions are honorable, I assure you."

She was already here, and she wouldn't get another chance. She had been surprised that his personal cabin wasn't the first stop. Perhaps because he had something to hide. "I would be delighted."

Captain Shaw held the door and gestured for her to enter. Julia stepped through and gasped at the sight. His quarters were twice the size of Branna's. Ostentatious didn't even begin to describe this cabin as she stepped carefully around the exotic animal hides dotting the floor. The furniture was leather, the tables gleaming exotic wood and iron, and the bed enormous and dressed with silk sheets and more animal hides. It was absurd.

He must have interpreted her speechlessness as a compliment as he showed her around, picking up various instruments to show her how they worked. He showed her curios from his travels and spoke proudly of his hunting.

Julia's head pounded and she worked not to massage her temples under the onslaught of his ridiculousness. She let her gaze sweep the room, looking for anything unoffensive on which to rest her gaze.

There against the bulkhead at the foot of the bed was a bolt lock. The same place a lock would have been if there was one on her office door in Branna's quarters. It was suspicious as she couldn't see a door. She moved to take a closer look and covered her movement by running her hand along the cool, smooth bed linens.

"Very nice, Captain," she purred and moved to the end of the bed. There was a door. She could just make out the outline of it. It was obviously built to be hidden. Her heart thumped wildly in her chest, and she clenched her fists to keep her hands from shaking. She needed to know.

She threw a teasing look over her shoulder at him. "Is this where you keep your riches, Captain?" She threw the bolt and opened the door.

She caught a flash of movement before the door slammed shut, Captain Shaw's meaty hand on it and his angry face looming over her.

"That room is off-limits, Miss Farrow," he said menacingly.

She flinched from his anger and that she didn't have to fake. "I'm sorry, Captain. I didn't realize."

"It is I who should apologize, Miss Farrow. You had no way of knowing and I'm sorry if I frightened you." He took up her hand and pulled her away from the door. "But since you asked." He stomped on one of the deck floorboards, making a hollow sound. "My riches, as you say, are most secure."

Julia eyed the floor and filed the information away. "I should go."

"Will I see you again?"

"I can assure you, Captain, you will."

There was a boat waiting to take her back to the *Banshee* and Captain Shaw kissed the back of her hand as he helped her over the gunwale. "I anxiously await our next meeting, Miss Farrow."

"As do I, Captain."

CHAPTER ELEVEN

Branna paced the deck, her body so tense it was painful. Julia had been gone for hours. It was too dark to see movement, but the night sky was bright enough to see the *Ferryman* was still in port. She had no reason to think anything had gone wrong, but her insides twisted with worry.

"There's a boat approaching," Nat called from the crow's nest.

Branna ran to the gunwale and waited, her hands gripping the wood. She heard the splash of the oars long before the boat came into view. She could just make out Julia in the bow and she let out a strangled breath of relief.

Julia climbed the ladder and fell into Branna's waiting arms, gripping Branna so tightly she thought her spine might snap.

Branna finally pulled away far enough that she could see her face. Her eyes and hands moved over Julia's body checking for injury. "Are you all right? Did he hurt you?"

"I'm fine, Branna. I'm fine. I'm okay. No one hurt me."

"Come with me." She pulled her toward the cabin.

Julia let Branna lead her along until she got through the door and then moved directly to the desk and uncorked the rum bottle. She tried to pour but her hands shook so much she spilled more than made it to the glass.

"Let me." Branna took the bottle from her and poured her a generous drink while Julia sat on the bed and dropped her head into her hands.

"Julia?"

"It's nothing. Just a headache." She gulped the drink Branna handed her with barely a wince.

"Another?"

Julia shook her head. "She's there, Branna. Bridget is there and she's alive, though not for much longer, I think."

"You saw her?"

"Just a flash of movement. I know it was a woman so who else would it be? She's locked in a room off the captain's quarters."

Branna breathed deeply, her fists clenched in anger. "Okay."

Julia winced and rolled her head. "I wish there was something I could have done. She was there and I just left her."

Branna moved behind her and dug her thumbs into the taut muscles of her neck and shoulders. "No, Julia. There was nothing more you could do. You did well. You found out what we needed to know."

"God, that feels good. What now?"

"I don't know yet. I need to talk to the crew and we're going to need help. I'll have to go back into town, maybe talk to the Swansboroughs again and find out who here is still loyal to them."

"I don't know if she has that much time, Bran."

She understood Julia's frustration, but they couldn't take on Captain Shaw on their own. He had too much support. They would have to find another way. "I know. We'll do everything we can, I promise."

Julia blew out a breath, all the fight leaving her. She reached behind her and plucked at the laces of her dress. "Will you help me undo these? They're tight."

Branna swiftly unlaced the back of Julia's dress. "How did you get it on?"

"Skill." She sucked in a deep breath, her first of the night.

Branna massaged her neck and shoulders again. "Did you bring that dress for me?"

"I did. I'm sorry, but I don't think you'll be seeing me in it again."

"I understand. You look stunning, by the way."

"Thank you. I'll get another one."

"Machree, you can wear whatever you like. Or nothing at all. You are beautiful to me no matter what."

"Thank you," Julia whispered and leaned back into Branna's hands.

Julia sat in the bow of the boat, arms wrapped around herself even in the warmth of the morning. She stared at nothing while Jack rowed her, Branna, Nat, and Gus to the docks. They needed to find help to defeat Captain Shaw and they needed to move fast. Bridget was in more danger than ever, and all Julia could think about was how frightened she must be.

Branna spoke quietly with Nat and Gus, though her gaze never traveled far from her. Julia knew she looked as poorly as she felt—drawn and pale. Her headache had eased for a while with Branna's help, but it had returned overnight and was sapping her strength.

Julia let Branna help her from the boat, grabbing up her skirt to keep it from getting tangled. She continued to dress in skirts and blouses, as much to follow Branna's original wish and also because it was simply more comfortable. She kept her boots with a dagger tucked away as it gave her a semblance of protection.

She stood on the dock and squinted into the morning sun, shielding her eyes as her head pounded anew. If only she could relax, she knew the pain would ease but there didn't seem a chance of that anytime soon. Not as long as they were under threat of Captain Shaw.

Branna, Nat, and Gus had headed into town and had been gone nearly an hour while Julia continued to hover aimlessly around their cargo. She wasn't sure what she was supposed to be doing. She had been tasked with staying around the docks with Jack and keeping their eyes and ears out to find out any information they could use against Captain Shaw.

Julia knew Branna just didn't want her along while she, Gus and Nat went into town to try and find the woman, Mary, and muster some help in driving Captain Shaw out of Port Royal. Julia was on the ragged edge, and she knew she wouldn't be much help. Branna knew it, too.

She wandered around, continuing to eavesdrop on conversations but knew they were not at all helpful. All she heard were the dockworkers grumbling. If anyone thought her presence there was odd, no one challenged her.

At the far end of the dock Jack was engaged in conversation with a couple of men. He looked up at her and gave her a wave. Julia started another circuit around the cargo crates from their ship when a hand gripped her arm. The hand was attached to a thin, filthy boy.

"Are ya…are ya Julia?" he stammered.

"Yes." Her skin prickled with alarm.

"Cap'n Kelly is in trouble. Ya have ta come, miss."

"What? What happened?" She looked up for Jack. He was still at the end of the dock and not paying any attention to her.

"Come now, miss." He started to trot back to the path leading to town.

"Jack! Branna is in trouble!" She didn't wait and took off down the dock after the boy, relieved to hear thundering steps and Jack calling after her.

Julia wanted to let Jack catch up, but the boy was so quick as he led her into town and through a maze of paths and alleyways. She turned the corner into the alley she thought he had ducked down and skidded to a stop when she couldn't see him anymore.

The alley was deserted but for rats scuttling through the rotting food and trash. Her heart hammered and the hair stood up on her arms. She had made a terrible mistake. Branna wasn't down here. She heard Jack calling her name, but he sounded far away, and she ran back to the mouth of the alley. A dark figure loomed in front of her, and she slammed into the rock-hard chest of a man twice her size.

"Miss Farrow." His voice rumbled as an enormous hand clamped down hard on her shoulder. "You need to come with me."

"No!" Julia screamed and struggled against his grip. "Jack!"

The man grunted his displeasure and spun her around, his thick forearm closing around her neck, effectively silencing her.

Terror gripped her and she kicked wildly and pulled at the arm cutting off her air. "Jack…"

"I'm not supposed to hurt you."

His words sent her into a near panic, her vision starting to gray, as she continued to struggle. "No…"

"Captain," Jack yelled as he burst into the office behind the bar.

Branna spun from her conversation with Mary at Jack's alarming entrance. "Jack?"

"It's Julia. She's gone."

"Gone where?"

"I don't know. It was a trap. I think she was taken. I'm sorry. She took off so fast and I couldn't find her."

"You, come with us," she barked at Mary as she charged out the door.

Branna thundered down the docks, her men following closely behind with Mary in tow. Out in the harbor she could see the *Ferryman* well enough. There were men scrambling up the shrouds and more turning the capstan to bring up the anchor.

"Goddamnit!" she screamed and jumped in the boat as the rest of them piled in. Two men to an oar and they were back at the *Banshee* in minutes.

Branna raced to her cabin and grabbed the sextant and a chart of the waters around Port Royal and ran back on deck, vaulting onto the quarterdeck and training the spyglass on the increasingly smaller *Ferryman*.

Her mouth was dry and blood roared in her ears. Not again. Not again. She unrolled the chart and pinned it to the compass table as the wind began to whip around her, threatening to blow the chart away. The sky was darkening and clouds rolling in, blotting out the sun. A storm.

She leveled the sextant at the ship and took note of its course while the men turned the capstan of the *Banshee*. Her crew were poised in the rigging, ready to unfurl the sails as soon as the anchor was up.

"Captain?" Jack said.

"Mr. Massey," she said, trying to rein in her rage. Captain first. Captain first.

"There was a boy and I think he told her you were in trouble. I was too far away, and I couldn't stop her."

His worry was clear. He would be an easy target for her rage, but she could see plainly how scared he was and how much he cared for Julia. They all did. "You couldn't have stopped her, Jack. Not if she thought I was in danger."

"It's my fault."

She needed her crew now more than ever. She needed Jack to focus. "It's that filth Shaw's fault. Look at me." She waited for him to raise his eyes. "We'll get her back."

"Aye, Captain."

They were interrupted by a shout from the capstan crew, screeching metal and a deep groan of the hull.

"Track them." Branna thrust the instruments at Jack before she jumped down to the deck and raced to the bow. Gus and Nat were peering over the side.

"What?" she barked. "What now?"

"The anchor's caught," Gus said. "We need a diver."

Branna didn't even wait for him to finish before jerking her scabbard over her head, dropping her knife belt and kicking off her boots. She grabbed the metal pike from Nat's hands and launched herself over the bow, entering the water in a sharp dive.

The salt stung her eyes, but she didn't need to see to pull herself along the chain thirty feet to the bottom and find the anchor wedged between two rocks. She jammed the pike beneath the heavy iron and rocked it back and forth until it snapped. Fortunately, not before dislodging a rock and freeing the anchor.

Her lungs burned and head pounded as she broke she surface, coughing and gasping for air. She lifted a trembling arm out of the water and swirled her hand. "Bring it up."

The capstan turned again, and she swam around to the side of the ship and hauled herself up the ladder they dropped for her.

Gus was there to hand her a cloth and dry clothes. She stripped out of her wet clothes on the deck, re-dressed and went in search of her boots and weapons.

"Where is she?" Branna asked, looking to the horizon where she had last seen the ship.

"We still have her in our sights," Gus assured her.

"The storm will be on us soon and they won't have gone far. They'll have to take shelter somewhere and I have an idea where they're headed. I want us faster."

"Captain?"

"Dump everything that's not essential. All food stores and supplies. Anything we don't need for battle."

"Aye aye."

The capstan ground to a halt and Nat's voice rang out orders across the deck. The sails were raised and filled immediately in the increasing wind. The *Banshee* surged into motion, nearly knocking Branna off her feet. They would give chase, and Branna would not rest until Julia was safe.

Julia's throat was on fire and her head felt like it had been split in two, far too big for her shoulders. There was a cool cloth on her face and a woman's soft humming. "Branna…"

"No. I'm sorry, love. It's only me."

She cracked her eyes and tried to focus. Bridget Bennett leaned over her and ran a cloth across her brow. "Bloody hell," she groaned, hoarsely, as the memory of what happened came rushing back and she surged up.

"Slowly," Bridget said with concern and helped her to sit. "I'm sorry I couldn't move you somewhere more comfortable. Are you all right?"

Julia prodded the tender skin around her neck and swallowed painfully a few times. "Water?"

Bridget handed her a glass, and Julia took a few swallows. It soothed some of the ache in her throat.

"Bridget, we've been looking for you."

"You were with Captain Kelly the other night."

"Julia Farrow."

"I remember. So, you've come to rescue me?"

"How am I doing?"

Bridget sat back against the wall and propped her hands on her knees. "I'd say we're both in a fair amount of trouble." She paused as the ship rolled. "We're at sea, love."

"Bloody hell," she muttered. Captain Shaw would never steal her and then wait around to see what happened. He'd set sail, no doubt, to put some distance between him and the *Banshee*.

She pushed herself to her feet. She was in the room off the captain's quarters. It was small and spare. A narrow bed, a table with fresh water, a lantern, a bucket, and not much more.

"It's not much to look at," Bridget said dryly. "But it's home."

Julia barked a laugh. "The last time I was captive on a ship I was chained in the hold with rotting corpses."

"Dear, God."

"I'm sorry. Forget I said that."

"I'll try."

"We won't be here long, anyway." Julia felt around the crack in the door.

"Branna will come for you."

"Branna will come for both of us." The thought of Branna caused Julia's chest to tighten. She must be going wild. "But we're not waiting for her." Julia slid the knife from her boot, immensely grateful Branna had insisted that she present herself as less capable than she was, as they clearly hadn't searched her when they brought her aboard.

The dagger was just thin enough and Julia worked the blade between the door and the wall. She slid it up slowly until she felt the resistance against the bolt. She applied a little pressure to maintain contact between the two metals and moved the dagger blade from side to side.

The bolt was well maintained and moved easily in its bracket, but she could only move it a small fraction at a time. It was tedious and before long her hands were cramped, and her head pounded from the effort.

A door slammed open on the other side and the sound of men's voices filled the room outside their door. Julia eased the blade out of the door and back into her boot. She looked at Bridget. "Do they speak freely in there?"

Bridget shrugged. "I suppose they think I'm either too stupid to understand or not in any position to do anything about it. They'd be right about the latter."

Julia pressed her ear to the door, though she didn't need to. She could hear them quite clearly.

"This storm came out of nowhere."

"No matter. It will be just as bad for them, and we have a good lead on them. Sail into it."

"Captain?"

"We'll head to the island northwest of Port Royal, where we last made repairs. The cove there will offer us protection from the winds and the worst of the rains."

"Kelly will head there too in this weather. It's the only safe place."

"I'm counting on it. We'll lay in wait and put her on the ocean floor as soon as she's within range."

"She'll be expecting a fight. You know what happened to Jag—"

"Of course, she will, but she won't fire on us."

Julia shuddered at the sound of the captain's laughter and her rage grew. He was using her to draw Branna in. He would hide behind her. Branna would never risk firing on this ship if she thought Julia was on it. She had to find a way to thwart his plan and give Branna a fighting chance. To do that she had to take herself out of the equation.

The bolt slid open and Julia backed away when Captain Shaw entered. "Miss Farrow, I'm so pleased you are well."

Julia backed away. "Keep away from me."

He frowned. "I'm sorry for the way you arrived here. Angus sometimes doesn't realize what a brute he can be. I trust Miss Bennett has been taking good care of you?"

"You're a dead man, Captain Shaw," Bridget snapped.

He turned angry eyes to her. "Oh? By whose hand?"

"Captain Kelly will see you dead for what you've done."

Julia tried to catch Bridget's eye to signal her to silence.

In two quick strides, his hand closed around Bridget's neck and lifted her to her toes.

"No!" Julia threw jabbing punches into his lower back as Jack had taught her. "Let her go!"

He grunted and loosened his grip, dropping Bridget to the floor. "Enough! You'll injure yourself." He caught her clenched fist in his hand and examined the reddening skin over her knuckles.

The man was well and truly mad. Julia jerked her hand free. "Let go of me."

"I'm afraid there is a storm, and my presence is needed on deck. When we get through this, I promise, my dear, I will make it up to you."

The bolt slid home and Julia groaned, flexing her sore hands. She pulled the knife from her boot.

Bridget had pulled herself up against the wall and massaged her bruised neck. "Thank you."

"I think it best we don't antagonize him further," Julia said and got to work on the lock.

CHAPTER TWELVE

Branna entered her cabin. They were at full sail, plunging through the increasingly choppy water and growing swells. The sea was littered with crates and sacks as the crew threw unnecessary cargo overboard to lighten the ship. There was nothing more she could do on deck.

She headed straight for her navigation table and unrolled the chart she had collected from the quarterdeck to keep from getting wet.

"Captain Kelly?"

Branna looked up, startled. She had completely forgotten about Mary in their frantic departure. She sat hunched on the edge of Branna's bed and looked terrified. "Mary, are you all right?"

"What's happening?"

"Captain Shaw has headed out to sea and we're giving chase. I'm sorry, I shouldn't have brought you here. I thought, perhaps, you could help before I realized what was going on."

"No. I want to be here. I'll help anyway I can."

Branna held out a hand for her. "Come with me."

Mary let Branna lead her through to the office. "You can stay in here. You'll be safe and Julia won't mind if you use her cabin."

"Julia's cabin? I thought you two were…"

"We are. She needs her own space to work, and dare I say, get away from me from time to time." She laughed softly but her chest tightened painfully. Julia was in real danger and Branna was so far away.

"Oh. Okay, good."

"What does that mean?"

"Nothing. It's just, for a moment I thought maybe, I thought maybe…nothing, it's silly."

"You don't have anything to worry about, Mary."

"Bridget still talks about you," she said softly, though there was no judgment or accusation in her voice. "She cares about you a great deal."

"And I her. You love her, don't you?"

"Very much."

"I'm glad. She deserves to have someone special in her life. We'll get her back."

"Please, let that be true, Captain."

Branna was still hunched over the navigation table when someone knocked. "Come."

Gus entered. "Captain, the men are awaiting your orders."

Branna didn't acknowledge him and continued to stare blankly at the chart, her gaze flicking over it, her shoulders tense.

"We're not more than a couple of hours from the island. The storm is moving fast, and it's already raining like the end of days. How do you want to go at them?" Gus asked.

The rain had been pounding outside her window for some time and she hadn't even noticed. Nothing registered, nothing made sense.

"Branna, Julia needs you. You must think clearly."

"I don't know. God, help me, I don't know what to do."

"Captain Shaw is expecting us."

"Aye." She had considered sailing all the way around the island and coming in from the other side, but even if they didn't smash to pieces on the rocky shoreline, it would take more time than Branna was willing to give.

"He thinks he has our hands tied. He thinks with Julia on board we won't act against him," Gus said.

"He's right."

"No. All we have is the element of surprise. What's the last thing he'll expect from us?"

"He won't expect us to fire."

"Right. He'll wait for us to come in close, waiting to take his best shot because he thinks we're not going to fire."

"We're not. Not with Julia on board."

"Damn it, Branna. We must. Are you just going to sail in there and let him blow us out of the water? Think for a minute. Julia knows you and knows this ship. She'll get somewhere safe if she can. She would never let you sacrifice yourself or the ship or any of us for her and you know that."

"I don't know where she is. I won't risk her."

"Let's assume she's with Bridget. Where was that?"

"The captain's cabin." They could fire to disable, not destroy. They could keep the barrage away from the quarterdeck.

Branna studied the charts with renewed interest, her mind running through the possibilities. She knew she was an excellent strategist and if anyone could defeat Captain Shaw and the *Ferryman*, it was her. As long as she could maintain her focus—and her resolve.

"I've almost got it," Bridget exclaimed as she continued to work the blade against the bolt.

Julia watched her anxiously. They had been at it for hours with Bridget relieving her from time to time so she could work the cramps out of her hands. "Wait. Don't unlock it all the way."

"Why not? I thought we were getting out of here."

"And go where?" Julia paced, running through the plan in her head. "If we leave now, we have nowhere to go. They'll tear the ship apart looking for us and we'll never get another chance."

"What then? Why are we doing this?"

"We *are* getting out of here. Just not yet. We must wait until we're closer to land. You heard the captain. He's taking the ship to a protected inlet to wait out the storm and wait for Branna. If there's to be the protection he seeks, we'll have to be close to land. We'll go then."

"Okay. And what do we do until then?"

Julia paced again. "Before we go, we have to disable the ship."

Bridget laughed. "How the hell are we going to do that, love?"

"I don't know yet." She *did* know that she wasn't just going to let Branna sail into an ambush. She had some time. She would think of something. She just needed to clear her mind and stop being so frantic. A solution would come.

Julia sat on the floor against the bulkhead and drew her legs up, resting her hands over her knees. She closed her eyes and let the dramatic pitching and rolling of the ship lull her into relaxation. They didn't have long. The island northwest of Port Royal was a well-known haven for ships on this route. With any luck there would be other ships there waiting out the storm that could assist them.

"Julia?" Bridget called from a similar position on the floor on the opposite side of the room.

"Hmm?"

"Will you talk to me?"

Bridget was pale, her mouth tight with strain. She looked terrified, and at present Julia was not helping to ease her mind, so lost was she in her own thoughts. Or, more accurately, in her attempts not to think at all. "Of course."

Bridget swallowed heavily a few times and looked for a moment like she might be ill. "How will you know when it's time? When we've come to the island?"

Julia stared at her for a long moment until she realized Bridget really had no idea. The ship chose that moment to drop so gut-churningly into a trough even Julia swallowed hard. "The island will offer protection from these swells. The wind will have lessened considerably, and the water will be far less rough. We'll know."

"Oh. Of course."

"You've not spent much time at sea, have you?"

"No. Hardly ever. I can't even swim."

"Sorry. What?"

"I can't swim." Bridget smiled sheepishly and went on oblivious to Julia's alarm. "I bet you're wondering how Branna and I ever made a go of it at all."

"Bloody hell," Julia breathed and raked her hands through her hair.

"What? What's wrong?"

"How the bloody hell did you think we were going to get off this ship?"

"A boat?"

"There's no way. We can't let them see us. We must jump and swim to shore. It's our only chance."

Bridget's eyes filled with tears. "I'm sorry. You should just leave me."

Julia was immediately ashamed of the way she had spoken. None of this was Bridget's fault. There was no excuse for making her feel guilty. "Bridget, I'm sorry."

Julia moved over, staggering once as the ship lurched again, before sliding back down to sit next to her. She slipped an arm around the woman's shoulders and pulled her close. "I'm sorry, I didn't mean to speak harshly. I'm a strong swimmer and I can get us both there. We can look for a scrap of wood or a barrel to help." And just like that an idea took root in the back of her mind.

They sat in silence for some time until the wind lessened, and the violent rolling of the ship eased.

"It's time." Julia pulled the dagger from her boot and held it out to Bridget. "Care to do the honors?"

Bridget slipped the blade back in the door and worked the bolt again. She only worked at it for a few short minutes, neither of them daring to breathe, when the bolt slid free with a click.

Julia cracked the door and peered into the cabin. As expected, it was empty. She was gambling on the men being busy crewing the ship and preparing to battle the *Banshee*.

She ducked back into the room and hurried to the bunk, stuffing the few pillows beneath the blanket and arranging them to look as much like a sleeping person as she could. It would fool no one for long.

"What are you doing?" Bridget asked. "Aren't we leaving?"

Julia gripped her by the arms. "I'm leaving. Only for a little while and I'll be back for you. I'm going to lock the door behind me."

"No!"

"Listen to me. I need to move fast, and I can do that better on my own. I need to disable the ship. If someone comes looking for us, and I don't think they will, but if the captain comes in here, you tell him I'm unwell. Sit at the edge of the bed and pretend you're tending to me. Demand that he leaves us alone. Do you understand?"

"You won't leave me?"

"No. But I need you to buy me some time if he comes."

"What if he doesn't believe it?"

Julia pointed to the dagger in Bridget's hand. "Then you defend yourself."

Julia believed that Bridget could do what she must to survive and protect them. Now the question was, could *she*? She crept out of the room and slid the bolt back across.

CHAPTER THIRTEEN

Though only midafternoon, the sky was so dark it seemed nearer to night when Julia slipped through the door beneath the quarterdeck. Men slogged through water pooling on the deck, wiping rain out of their faces as they tended the lines and kept the ship on course. She suspected the captain, and perhaps Angus, were above her on the quarterdeck. She spared a glance over the starboard side, and even through the gloom and sheeting rain she could see land. They were close. They could make it.

No one seemed to notice one more person hunched against the storm, and she quickly ducked down the ladder belowdecks and moved fast through the corridors. She had an excellent memory and sense of direction and had paid particular attention to the layout of the ship in case she needed to describe to Branna where Bridget was being held.

Now she wanted the gun deck. She needed to get there before the captain called the men to their stations. She had no idea how far behind them Branna was, but she knew she didn't have long. She was not yet sure what she was going to do, but her best chance of crippling the ship would be from wherever there was a supply of gunpowder.

She slowed at the hatch to the gundeck. She heard the thump of barrels and scrape of metal. Someone was in there. She chanced a look in and saw only one man. He wasn't that much larger than her, and she could take him by surprise. She was doing this for Branna. To protect the *Banshee* and the people, she knew she would do whatever she must.

She peeked in the room again and waited until his back was turned. He appeared to be loading the cannons. There was a hiss as he poured gunpowder into the chamber and then stuffed the wadding into the bore with a long pole. Finally, he hefted a round and dropped it down. The cannon was loaded, and he moved on to the next.

On the ground just inside the door was another loading pole. It was thick and almost too heavy, but she didn't have time to look for something else. She waited until he lifted another small barrel of gunpowder before approaching him as quietly as possible.

"Who's there?" He turned, his eyes going wide. He was just a boy.

She hesitated, giving him time to drop the barrel and reach for his blade. He had the blade partially unsheathed when Julia swung at his head, connecting with a sickening crack and sending him sinking to the ground without another sound. She stood over him, poised for another strike but he wasn't getting up anytime soon.

She crouched next to him and placed the back of her hand under his nose. He was still alive. She unbuckled his belt and tightened it around her own waist, sliding his knife into the sheath.

There were shouts from the deck and booted feet overhead. The *Banshee* could be in sight. They could be sending the crew down to the gundeck. She needed to hurry.

She had originally thought to ignite a barrel of gunpowder and she considered the impressive supply in front of her. Stacked barrels filled an entire bulkhead, floor to ceiling. One barrel would ignite two and then… There was no way to control an explosion like that and she could incinerate the entire ship in the blink of an eye. She eyed the cannons and the track they slid out on when the gun port was open. At rest the guns sat several meters back from the hull. What would happen if she fired it inside? She tried to imagine the size of the hole it would blow in the hull and decided to light the two she knew to be loaded.

She couldn't leave the unconscious young man helpless where he had fallen and gripped him under the arms, dragging him across the floor and out into the corridor. She wasn't a murderer and she had already blindsided him once. He at least deserved a fighting chance.

The man was working by lantern light, and she raised the glass to reach the flame with a scrap of wood from a crate. She had no idea how long the fuse burned and how much time she would have to get out of the way.

She lit the wood from the lantern and held the small flame in front of her, sending up a silent prayer that she would get through this alive, before touching the flame to the two fuses in rapid succession. A burning hiss told her they had caught, and she ran for the door, making it out to the corridor before the world exploded.

She was thrown off her feet as the explosion of the two cannons firing inside the hull deafened her. There was a sharp pain in her left ear, and the heat and pressure change knocked her senseless and into the opposite bulkhead.

Smoke and the acrid smell of gunpowder filled the enclosed space and she coughed, as she struggled to her feet. She couldn't hear anything but ringing, and the floor seemed to tilt beneath her, her balance shaky. She touched a hand to her painful ear, and it came away sticky with blood.

"Bloody hell," she rasped when she caught a glimpse of the damage through the smoke—a jagged hole in the port side from the waterline to the gundeck, at least six feet wide, gaped in front of her. Water rushed in and the boat listed dangerously. She wanted to cripple them, and from what she could tell, she had sunk them. And she was on borrowed time.

She raced from the room and crept back onto the deck, narrowly missing being seen by a line of crew racing belowdecks to find out the source of the explosion and check the damage. Julia pressed herself against the wall and waited for them to pass. The deck was complete chaos with crew shouting and running across the dangerously listing ship. The ship was lost. They just didn't know it yet.

Julia moved back to the captain's quarters feeling no satisfaction in her success. They still had a long way to go to safety. She slid the bolt off the door to the locked room and raced in only to be thrown off her feet, a knife to her throat.

"Julia!" Bridget gasped and moved off her. "Oh, my God, I thought for sure you were dead!"

Julia shook her head and winced. She could see Bridget was talking to her, but it sounded like she was underwater. She pointed to her ear. "I can't hear you."

"You're bleeding."

"I'm okay." Though the pain in her ear was excruciating, her legs and arms still worked and at the moment that was all that mattered. "We have to go. Now."

Julia no longer cared who could see them. They raced out onto the deck and were nearly thrown overboard when the ship groaned and listed farther into the water. Men were shouting incoherently. Several were trying unsuccessfully to lower the boat while others were willing to take their chances on the swim and jumped over.

Julia banged up against the starboard gunwale and looked out. Though rain continued to pour, and the wind whipped wildly, the beach was even closer than she'd expected, maybe one hundred meters. The water churned below them but as she'd hoped there was plenty of debris from which to choose to aid them to shore.

"Climb up here," she yelled to Bridget to be heard over the storm and the panicking crew. She helped Bridget up to the gunwale and kicked off her boots, climbing up after her. She checked that the knife belted at her waist was secure. She was worried she was going to need it.

"Julia!" Captain Shaw screamed her name and it cut across the storm.

Julia spun and saw Captain Shaw charging her. She grabbed Bridget's hand. "Whatever you do don't let go of me."

The *Banshee* surged around the point and came into the cove. Branna and Gus stared at the sight in front of them. The *Ferryman* canted dangerously to port, her masts now at nearly a forty-five-degree angle to the water, her sails dragging. She was taking on water fast and the ship was most certainly doomed. Thick, black tendrils of smoke curled up from below and hung heavily in the damp air over the ship.

"What the hell?" Gus shouted.

Branna snatched the spyglass and jammed it to her eye. She could just make out the top of the hole in the hull as the ship sank lower with every passing second. The men still on deck were frantic, some trying futilely to right the lines, some cowering and clinging to the ship and some still going over the side. The water was littered with wreckage and floundering crewmen.

"Jesus Christ."

"Can you tell what happened?"

If Julia and Bridget were locked in the ship, they would surely drown when the ship went under. She jerked the spyglass around the deck. There. Julia was on the gunwale with Bridget, preparing to jump. They looked okay and Julia was armed, and the pieces clicked into place. Branna exhaled. "Julia Farrow happened."

Gus let out a bark of laughter. "That's our girl."

They were far from out of danger. She raised the spyglass again in time to see Julia and Bridget jump, just as Captain Shaw lunged for them. Her blood roared in her ears. "Get me the new crewman! The crazy helmsman."

"Harris!" Gus bellowed and a young man scrambled down from the main mast, slipping down the shrouds and skidding across the deck in his rush to attend to the captain and first mate.

"Aye, Captain?" He pushed drenched hair from his face.

Branna pointed to the beach where Julia would be headed. "Take the wheel. Head us straight for the beach. We're dropping the boat at full sail."

"Captain?" Gus asked, alarmed.

"It will work. Take us in as close as you can as fast as you can, then hard to port. Preferably before you run us aground. Come back around and drop all but the main sail. Do *not* drop the anchor. Pick up any of Shaw's crew only under condition of full surrender and lock them in the hold. If they have a problem with that leave them to fend for themselves in the sea. Do you understand your orders, Mr. Harris?"

"Aye, aye, Captain." He scrambled up to the quarterdeck to take the wheel from Gus. The ship groaned as he turned her sharply toward the beach, heading straight for land.

"Mr. Hawke, Mr. Hooper, and Mr. Massey with me," she yelled and jumped down to the deck. The boat swung wildly on its ropes as the *Banshee* surged through the breaking swells toward land. She wanted more men, but for the stunt she was about to try, lighter would be better. "What do you think? Get in now and lower the boat or lower the boat first?" she asked.

Jack shook his head, looking over the side at the water crashing against the hull. "This is insane."

"Get in now," Nat and Gus answered in unison.

"Agreed," Branna said.

The four of them scrambled into the boat, staggering and banging into each other as it swayed wildly in its lines before they found their footing. Nat and Gus pushed hard off the gunwale and the arm swung out over the sea.

Brewer, Caswell, and Davy, looking uncharacteristically concerned, waited nearby to lower the boat at her command.

"Lower us just over the water. Wait for my command to cut us loose!" Branna yelled over the wind and roaring waves.

The men did as they were told and the boat jerked and dropped a few feet at a time until they were dangling just out of the water, spray lashing them in the face. Branna watched as the beach grew nearer. Wind whipped her hair and her clothes plastered to her body with rain and sea spray. Her sword dug painfully into her back and pulled at her shoulder as she sat hunched over and tried to protect herself from the worst of the deluge.

The *Banshee* surged closer to land and Branna raised her arm. As the ship groaned under the strain of a hard turn to port the boat swung crazily against the lines. Branna dropped her arm. "Cut us loose!"

They crashed into the water, the four of them hunkered low for balance and to keep from capsizing. The momentum from the ship had them rocketing through the swells as Jack wrestled to get the oars in the water. They were almost jerked out of his hands as, alone, he couldn't keep up with how fast they were already moving.

They shifted around, two to an oar and fell into a fast rhythm, pulling the boat the rest of the way to the beach.

CHAPTER FOURTEEN

Julia gripped the jagged plank of wood Bridget was partially draped across, her hand aching and abraded from slivers cutting into her water-softened skin. The beach was close, and she put on a renewed charge to get them out of the water. Her muscles trembled with exertion, her head foggy as she battled the breaks to kick them the remaining twenty yards.

A swell claimed them not far from the beach, all but throwing them the rest of the way. Julia coughed and spat seawater, dragging herself through the wet sand over to Bridget. She lay still, breathing raggedly, her face coated in wet sand.

"Come on, Bridget, we need to go." Julia got an arm around her and hauled her to her feet, the two of them staggering up the beach out of the water toward the tree line.

Julia dragged wet hair from her face and looked back, hope surging within her where before there was only fear. The *Ferryman* was partially submerged, crewmen still floundering in the water and some bodies already washing up on shore. Around her, though, sailed the *Banshee*. Strong and whole and the most beautiful thing she had ever seen.

"Bridget, look!" she shouted right before a vicious blow to her temple sent her to her hands and knees with a cry of pain.

"Julia!" Bridget screamed.

Julia swallowed down the urge to vomit. Her vision blurred and blood streamed down the side of her face, dripping onto the sand beneath her.

"I was hoping you'd survive that swim," a man snarled and jerked her to her feet with a hand knotted into the hair at the back of her neck. "You didn't really think Shaw cared what I did with those two little Bennett brats, did you? He bloody gave 'em to me."

Julia gasped as Captain Moore's face swam into view, his blade scraping against the skin of her throat.

"Thought I was a goner there for a while, what with not being able to swim. Good thing blowing a fucking hole in the ship left so many scraps of wood floating around. Been meaning to get some payback for gettin' my men kill—"

He grunted and his grip on her relaxed, the knife dropping away. Julia staggered away from him as he fell.

Moore lay on the beach making strange gurgling sounds, his hands covering a wound in his side, blood pouring through his fingers. Bridget stood over him, her eyes dark with rage, Julia's dagger in her hand dripping with blood.

"That's for Anna. And this is for Lilly." She plunged the knife into his throat. Blood sprayed across the sand then slowed to a trickle as he sucked in a ragged breath and stilled forever.

Julia blinked, unsteady on her feet, and felt a hand go around her waist. "We need to get out of here," Bridget said.

"No. Branna…Branna is here."

"There's no time, Julia!" Bridget shouted and pointed to the beach.

Branna and the others were in sight as they battled the boat to shore. At the shoreline though, a large figure crawled out of the water and stood, his mouth twisting into a malevolent smile.

Shaw was coming for them. Branna wouldn't get here in time. Julia grabbed Bridget's hand and they staggered into the jungle.

They were still ten meters out when Branna turned in time to see Julia take a hard blow from Captain Moore and go down. "Julia!" Branna shouted and grabbed at the oars again, pulling for all she was worth. Something tore in her gut, sending streaking pain through her middle. She ignored it as they continued to race to shore.

When she checked again, Moore lay unmoving in the sand and Julia and Bridget crashed blindly into the trees while Captain Shaw stalked up the beach and disappeared into the jungle after them. "Fucking bastard!"

The boat ground to a stop in the sand and Nat, Gus, and Branna jumped out and pushed the boat back into deeper water against the crashing waves. "Get back to the ship and bring more men," Branna ordered Jack. She couldn't count on help anytime soon. It took four of them to make it to the beach in the stormy water. Jack on his own may not make it at all.

"Aye, aye, Captain." Jack heaved on the oars, the boat shooting straight up and over the next swell before settling back down in the trough.

"Did you see where they went?" Gus asked as he studied the tree line.

"Aye," Branna said through her clenched jaw. She took a step up the beach and spun at an inhuman bellow of rage from their left.

"Oh, hell. Him," Gus muttered. Angus was charging down the beach like a raging bull, sword drawn.

Nat drew his sword. "Go, Captain. We'll take care of this."

Nat and Gus stood shoulder to shoulder, and Gus grinned. "We'll catch you up when we're through. It shouldn't be long."

Branna didn't wait to see what happened next and charged through the trees where she had seen Julia go in.

All Julia could hear was the roaring of blood in her ears and the sound of her own ragged breathing as they struggled through the thick foliage. Their directionless escape was hampered by mud, sodden clothes, and bare feet. She dropped to her knees with a cry when a jagged rock cut into the sole of her left foot.

"Julia, are you all right?" Bridget asked. "Christ, you're a mess, love. Here, let me see."

Julia leaned back on her hands and extended her leg, anxious about stopping, but grateful for the rest to catch her breath. Her head was splitting and her vision still wavered. "I'll be okay in a minute. We shouldn't stay long."

"You're hurt." Bridget prodded the puncture at the arch of her foot. She ripped a sleeve from her blouse and wound it twice around Julia's foot, tying it off.

"I've had worse."

"You and Branna have had some real adventures, haven't you?"

Julia barked a hysterical laugh. "Is that what you call this?"

"No. Right now it's bloody terrifying. If we live through it, it will have been an adventure."

"That's fair," Julia agreed, her breathing having finally returned to manageable. She was fit with the constant sailing and added training, but they had been climbing steadily, which would explain why she was so winded. "How are you doing?"

"I'm bloody done in. But I'm in one piece which is more than I can say for you." She parted Julia's hair and winced at the gash on her head.

"Miss Farrow!" Captain Shaw's voice boomed from down the hill followed by the sounds of him plowing through the growth after them.

Bridget jumped to her feet. "He sounds close. But I can't see anything."

Julia struggled upright and tested out her foot. The pain was sharp, and she could feel blood already soaking the makeshift dressing. She grabbed Bridget's hand. "We have to keep going."

The incline grew steep, and they struggled now as they slipped along the wet ground for several more minutes. Julia pushed through the bushes into a clearing as the ground finally levelled. There was thick brush on three sides and ahead the greenery was sparse. Julia ran toward the open space and skidded to a stop with a shout of fear as she came to the edge and peered over.

It was easily twenty meters down, jagged rocks and scrub brush the whole way before the jungle closed in again at the bottom. "No. No. No."

"This is bad, isn't it?" Bridget said from behind her.

She pushed Bridget back from the edge. "We have to go back."

"Miss Farrow," Captain Shaw called and burst through the trees. "There you are."

Bridget paled visibly, a hand going to her chest.

Julia stepped in front of her and drew the blade from her waist, her arm trembling. Shaw didn't draw his sword but approached slowly, his hands held out from his sides and away from the pistol tucked into his belt. She knew little of firearms, but she did know that wet gunpowder was unpredictable. It could fire, fizzle, or explode with equal chance.

"Julia," he said as he drew closer. "May I call you Julia? There's still a chance for us. Come with me."

"You've lost, Captain Shaw," Julia said with more confidence than she felt. "Your ship is destroyed, your crew dead or captured and Captain Kelly is here on the island."

His face turned murderous for a moment before softening again. "I have gold, Julia. We can start over. Build a new ship together."

She shook her head, unable to believe what she was hearing. He was out of his mind. But if she could keep him distracted, she could give Branna a chance to find them. He was getting too close, and Julia lunged awkwardly at him. "Stay back!"

"Julia, please, put that down before you injure yourself," he said as if to a misbehaving child.

Her gaze darted around the clearing. There was a break in the trees to their left. Bridget could make it. She pulled Bridget over to her left, nearer the trees. "When I tell you, run."

"No, Julia, I'm not leaving you."

"Yes, you are. Back the way we came. Find Branna and tell her where I am." She didn't give Bridget another opportunity to argue and charged at the captain, slashing her blade wildly in the air in front of him. "Now!"

A scrabble of feet and crash of leaves let her know Bridget had done as she asked.

Captain Shaw's eyes widened in surprise at Julia's attack and he drew his sword. "Julia, what are you doing?"

The time for talk was over. She had had enough. She could never beat him, but she was tired of running and pretending she was less than she was. She was done being a victim. Rage filled her and lent her strength and she feinted to the right. He moved to parry her swing and she spun, slashing across his left side, cutting him across the ribs.

He staggered back, a hand going to the wound and coming away bright with blood. "You cut me."

She was unable to keep a satisfied smile from crossing her face. "I apologize, Captain, but I'm afraid I may have misled you."

His face purpled with rage, and he charged her, swinging his short sword and bringing it down like a club. "I will not be made a fool of."

When all his momentum was on his downswing, she ducked under his arm, slashing her blade across the back of his knee as she moved past him. "Seems you're doing a pretty good job of that all on your own."

He dropped to one knee, gripping his damaged leg and howling in pain.

Julia was tiring fast. Her injuries slowed her and sapped her strength. She caught her breath and wiped blood from her eye. Captain Shaw stood across the clearing from her, not ten yards away. He was bleeding steadily from the wound in his side and the back of his thigh, and he watched her warily. Neither injury was life-threatening, but they had weakened him.

She didn't know how much longer she could keep this up and risked a glance behind her. She could make a run for it back the way they came.

"You can't outrun me, Julia," he said.

Her attention snapped back to him and she tensed when his eyes narrowed. He was preparing to rush her again. Better to try and end this now. She lowered herself, her blade at the ready as he streaked across the clearing and came at her again, trying to overpower her with his size. She stepped into him, spinning through his swing and scoring her blade across his sword arm. His sword dropped uselessly from his hand and skidded away in the dirt.

He grunted in pain but was ready for her this time, lashing out with his left fist and connecting hard with her side as she tried to move out of reach.

The air left her lungs with a whoosh and she dropped to her hands and knees. She gathered her legs beneath her, but his foot whipped out, kicking her legs out from under her and sending her crashing onto her back, her own weapon skittering out of reach. Captain Shaw stood over her, his large form blotting out the storm. It was over.

CHAPTER FIFTEEN

Branna burst into the clearing to see Captain Shaw looming over Julia. Julia was moving but clearly injured. "You're a fucking dead man, Shaw."

"Captain Kelly, how nice of you to join us." He gripped Julia by the arm and pulled her roughly to her feet, snaking an arm around her waist to hold her close. He took a step back with her, nearing the edge of the cliff.

Julia's head lolled back against his chest, but her gaze focused on Branna. "I'm sorry."

Julia was a bloody mess. Shaw was in worse shape, blood pooling beneath him where he stood. "For what, machree?"

"I wasn't fast enough."

"You were incredible, and I couldn't be prouder. You're going to be all right."

"Well, isn't this touching," Shaw sneered and drew the pistol from his belt with his injured arm. He pointed it at Branna. "I think, though, our little reunion must come to an end."

Branna held her sword out to her side and moved forward another step.

"Stay where you are!" Shaw screamed.

"You swam to shore with that pistol. It will never fire."

"Care to wager your life on that?"

"Yes."

He moved the barrel to Julia's temple. "Care to wager hers?"

Branna froze. She didn't think that pistol would fire, but if the gunpowder had dried out it might. Or it could explode. Either way Julia could be killed. She ran through her options and didn't see many. She set her sword on the ground. "This is between you and me, Shaw. Let Julia go."

"On the contrary. Miss Farrow has some things to answer for." He cocked the hammer.

"No, don't! I'll do anything." Branna could barely draw a breath and her throat closed with fear.

Shaw grinned, triumphantly. "The great Captain Kelly, brought to her knees by the love of a woman. But since you offered, there is something you have that I want."

"Name it."

"Your ship."

Branna drew a ragged breath. "Done."

Shaw roared with laughter. "I understand you are an honorable woman, Captain. You will escort me back to the beach and you will ensure no one raises a hand against me. You will return my captured crewmen. I am not an unreasonable man. Your crew is free to remain with you or come with me. Do I have your word?"

"No," Julia cried, tears tracking through the blood and grime. "Branna, please, you can't."

"Julia, it's okay. You have my word, Shaw. Now, let her go."

"I want to trust you, Captain, but I believe I'll hold onto Miss Farrow a while longer."

Julia's expression darkened. "I won't let this happen."

Branna tensed. "Please, Julia, it's—"

"I love you, Bran. Always." She dug in her heels and kicked out, sending them both staggering back toward the cliff's edge. Shaw flailed out, the pistol flying from his hand as he tried to regain his balance and Julia propelled them past the point of no return.

"No!" Branna dove, wrapping her hand around Julia's wrist while Shaw went over with a scream, pulling at Julia's waist. Branna hit the ground, taking Julia's full weight and skidding toward the edge. There was a sickening pop and Julia screamed when her shoulder jerked beyond its limits.

The added weight of Captain Shaw was going to take them all over. With a final terrified howl, his grip loosened, and he fell away.

"Julia, hold on!" Branna's left hand clawed at the ground, finally clutching at a thin root system to stop her slide. "Julia. Julia, look at me."

Her head rolled at the sound of Branna's voice and her unfocused gaze met hers over the edge of the cliff. "Bran…"

"You have to take my hand."

"It hurts."

"I know it does. Please, Julia, just reach your left hand and grab onto me." Branna yelped as the roots gave under their combined weight and she slid closer to the edge.

"Let me go."

"Never. I'm never letting you go. Do you hear me? Now reach up and take my bloody hand. That's a bloody goddamn order."

Julia jerked her left arm up.

"That's it, Julia. Reach up. You can do it." Julia's left hand closed around Branna's arm.

"That's it," Branna exhaled when she felt Julia's hand tighten around her. She risked a shift and turned her head to face back into the clearing. "Gus! Nat! Help!"

Julia groaned. "I don't know how long…I can…"

"Don't you dare give up on me." Branna swallowed hard, desperately trying to think of something to keep Julia going. "I accidently brought Mary with us when we came after you. She loves Bridget very much and she was worried I was coming back for her."

"Oh, Bridget…"

"She's okay You saved her, Julia. She told me where to find you. I sent her to get Nat and Gus."

"Good...that's good..." Her grip on Branna loosened and her left arm fell away.

"Fuck! Julia, please, don't let go." She scrabbled frantically against the slide toward the edge before a hand closed like iron around her arm.

"I've got you, Branna," Gus grunted and pulled at Branna while Nat reached past them and dragged an unconscious Julia back up over the side and away from the edge.

"Julia." Branna sobbed and pulled her into her lap. She was frightfully pale, but her pulse beat strongly at her neck.

Gus laid a hand on her arm. "Captain, we have to go."

Branna nodded. "Can one of you—"

"I've got her." Nat gathered Julia into his arms.

Branna struggled to her feet with a gasp, pain streaking across her gut.

"Branna." Gus gripped her arm to steady her.

"I'm all right." She straightened with a wince. "I'm all right."

Julia woke to the soft crackling of a fire and nearby voices. She winced at the ache in her shoulder, her right arm was bound snugly across her chest, and her head throbbed in time with her pulse. Her left hand was immobile, too—her fingers laced tightly in another's grip.

"Julia." Branna let go of her hand and pushed herself up with grunt and a hand across her middle.

"Bran, what happened to you?"

"What happened to *me*? Have you seen yourself?"

"I can imagine." She probed gently at the side of her head, rough threads of stitches and greasy ointment. She touched her ear and winced.

"There was some blood, but we couldn't see an injury," Branna said.

"It happened when the cannons went off. I wasn't far enough away. I can't hear very well out of that ear," she said. She wiggled her toes and more stitches pulled at the skin of her injured foot.

"I'm afraid you're going to be out of commission again for a while."

Julia sighed deeply, exhausted physically and emotionally. "Did we get him?"

"You sure did. Julia, you were amazing. You fought him and you won."

She wasn't ready to think about what had happened, what she'd had to do to survive. "Is everyone okay? Nat? Gus?"

"Everyone is fine. A little banged up but fine, some new scars and missing teeth." Branna looked out across the beach. "Those fools are trying to reenact their fight with Angus so they can better tell the story later."

Julia followed Branna's gaze. Nat and Gus were moving around the beach and arguing with each other. "It looks like they're dancing."

"What can I get you?"

"Water or tea, maybe?"

Branna went into the shelter near the fire and returned a few minutes later with a warm mug of dark liquid. "Tea."

Julia took a sip and grimaced. "Tea?"

"The rum will ease your pain and help you rest."

"Branna, I'm okay," she insisted, but drank the mug of heavily spiked tea down anyway before dropping back against the pile of blankets.

Branna cupped Julia's cheek. "I love you. I don't know what I would have done if I had lost you."

Julia covered Branna's hand with her own. "You'll never have to find out."

Julia woke later. She was sweating under the blankets and so near the fire. Branna was not in the shelter. "Hello?"

Bridget sat down next to her. "How are you feeling, love?"

"Better, I think." She pushed herself up and waited a moment. There was no dizziness. "Where's Branna?"

Bridget nodded toward the beach. "The water in the cove has settled. They're going to dive the wreck and try and salvage some of the *Ferryman*."

"That sounds like her."

"Do you want to try and eat something? There's soup."

"Not yet, thank you." Mary was by the fire watching the crew work out around the wreck. The three of them were the only ones in the shelter. "I'd like to get cleaned up. Can you help me?"

"Mary," Bridget called. "I think they brought clothes for Julia from the ship. Can you look for them?"

Mary gathered up a stack of clean clothes, a cloth, soap, and pot of warm water. "I'm glad to see you're okay, Julia. Bridget told me what you did. I don't know how we can ever thank you."

"Seeing you both safe is thanks enough."

They managed to get Julia cleaned up and dressed in a clean skirt and soft, worn button-down shirt. Mary helped her get her feet into soft slippers to protect her bandaged foot and Bridget rewrapped her arm against her chest.

They walked slowly down the beach, the women steadying Julia when she wobbled in the soft sand.

Branna turned when she heard them approach. "What are you doing up?"

"I'm okay, Bran. I want to see how it's going." She shielded her eyes from the sun and leaned into the supporting arm Branna offered.

The storm had blown itself out and the waters, at least where they were protected, were calmer. The winds and rough seas had blown the wreck even closer to shore and the masts and part of the deck were visible above the waterline, the remnants of ragged sails flapping in the breeze.

The *Banshee* was anchored a little farther out and the boat bobbed nearby, Jack at the oars and Gus and Nat leaning over the side, hovering over the sunken ship. There were lines in the water and half a dozen crewmen floated at the surface before diving back down.

Julia shuddered at the sight of the once majestic ship now reduced to ruin by her hand. "Any luck?"

"Not sure yet. They spent the first couple hours pulling bodies out."

Julia gasped. "Oh, God."

"Julia, you are *not* responsible."

"How can you say that? How many survived?"

Branna looked away.

"How many?"

"We pulled twenty-three men from the water. Not all of them made it. The survivors are in the hold. We'll return them to Port Royal to be dealt with."

Julia groaned. "No. There were at least fifty crew on board."

"Julia, look at me. They were going to kill you and Bridget and all of us if they got the chance. You know that's true."

"I know. Captain Shaw didn't think you would engage him with me on board. He was waiting for you. He would have destroyed you."

"You saved us, Julia. You saved us all."

Julia exhaled. "Okay."

"Okay?" Branna asked.

Julia offered her a small smile. "No, not okay, but what else can I do?"

Branna pulled Julia close to her again and Julia relaxed her head against her shoulder. "The ship is in shallow-enough water that it's easy to get to but there isn't much salvageable. All food stores, firearms, and gunpowder are ruined. They've recovered some blades and hardware we can use. If he had any gold on the ship, we haven't been able to find it."

"Oh," Julia whispered.

"What? What's wrong?"

"I know where it is."

CHAPTER SIXTEEN

By the evening they had broken camp and returned to the *Banshee*. The water became too murky with their salvage, and they had not recovered the gold. Branna wanted to take one more crack at it in the morning when the sea floor had calmed.

She helped Bridget and Mary settle in Julia's office, cramped for two but they seemed happy enough to be close to one another. They, too, were feeling the effects of having nearly lost one another and were never more than a few feet apart.

Branna slid the door closed to give them privacy and sat at the edge of the bed where Julia rested. "You need to try and eat something."

Julia shook her head, drowsily. "Tomorrow."

Branna picked up her left hand, almost the only part of her that didn't seem battered in some way, and brushed her lips across the back of her hand. Her eyes burned with tears as she looked at Julia while she slipped her ring back onto her finger.

Julia squeezed her hand. "What's wrong?"

"What were you thinking?" Branna asked, unable to keep the edge of anger from her voice. The memory and fear of seeing Julia go over the cliff was still sharp in her mind and her heart. "Why would you do that?"

"He needed to be stopped, Branna. He would have hurt so many more people and you were going to give up everything for me."

"*You* are everything. None of this means anything anymore without you. If you ever pull a stunt like that again I will set this ship aflame myself."

"I understand, Captain."

"See that you do. I love you, Julia Farrow. Please, get some rest."

"I love you, Branna Kelly."

Branna stood on the deck in the morning while Gus and Nat made one last dive to the wreck. They had been down for a while, Jack peering over the side of the boat. There was a mass of bubbles at the surface moments before both their heads popped above the water, gasping for breath.

Gus shook hair out of his eyes and held up a line from the water. "We found it!" he shouted and pounced on Nat, dunking him with a laugh.

Branna was about to congratulate them when a small schooner rounded the inlet and sailed into the cove. She tensed and jumped up onto the gunwale. The ship was small and light but in good repair. There were no gun ports and none of the crew she could see on deck appeared to be armed.

Branna eyed them warily as they dropped their sails and floated a way off. An older brown-skinned man came to stand at their starboard side.

"Ahoy, the *Banshee*," he called with a local accent.

"Good morning." Branna sensed no threat, but the ship was unknown to her.

"Captain Kelly. I'm pleased to find you well. I'm Captain Easton. We saw you leave out of Port Royal yesterday. We were on our way to port to check on the Swansboroughs. I'm a longtime associate of theirs. When we were able to track them down, Miss Swansborough let us know what was going on." He eyed the wreck. "I assume that's the *Ferryman*."

"It is. It met with an unfortunate end."

Captain Easton remained expressionless, but his eyes were bright with pleasure. "Pity. Perhaps we can share a drink and you can tell me about it?"

"It's not my story to tell. But I'm sure you'll hear about it in due course."

"But for the storm we would have caught up with you sooner. Is your crew well?"

Branna flicked her gaze back to the cabin where Julia still slept. She would recover completely with time. "We will be, thank you."

"May we be of service in any way?"

"We've nearly finished our salvage and will be returning to Port Royal by tomorrow morning. If you wouldn't mind going on ahead and letting the Swansboroughs know what's happened here. We have several survivors of the *Ferryman* in our hold. I would be grateful if you could take them off my hands and return them to Port Royal to be dealt with."

"It would be my pleasure. I'll send men over to retrieve them directly."

* * *

"I know it will never make up for what you've lost, Elizabeth, but it will help return the Swansborough Company to its position and restore your reputation," Branna said.

They sat again in the Swansborough's residence in town. Elizabeth, Oliver, and Jeremy Bennett had returned from their plantation. Abigail Swansborough and the girls, Lilly and Anna, had remained at the rural property. The fresh air and wide-open spaces were helping to restore their health and spirits.

"Thank you, Branna. Oliver told us what you did with the money from the *Serpent's Mistress*, setting up a fund to help those harmed by Captain Jagger. I'll have Mary set up a similar arrangement with the gold from Captain Shaw. I assume you accepted payment for your crew and your efforts?"

"I did. He was very wealthy, and you will be able to do a lot of good with that gold."

"What will you do now?" Elizabeth looked between Branna and Julia. Julia had remained quiet, seemingly lost in her own thoughts and likely in a fair amount of pain.

"We'll stay tonight and have the ship restocked and head back to Nassau in the morning. We'll take it slow and make sure Shaw's associates have cleared out of these waters."

"I don't think you have much to worry about on that account. When Captain Easton shared the news of the *Ferryman* on the sandy bottom, and marched the survivors down the dock in chains, a dozen ships left port by suppertime. Thank you, Branna, for everything."

"I had little to do with it, but you're most welcome."

Elizabeth turned to Julia. "Julia, is there anything I can do for you?"

"No, thank you, Elizabeth. I'm just happy to have been able to help."

Branna rose, looking to Oliver. "Mr. Swansborough, are you sailing with us?"

"With your permission, Captain, I'd like to stay on a little longer here and see to my family and the business."

Branna clapped him on the shoulder. "I should expect nothing less, my friend." She held out her hand for Julia. "Are you ready?"

Julia hesitated. "Actually, Elizabeth, there is something you can help me with if I may stay on here this afternoon?"

"Of course. Whatever you need."

"Do you mind, Bran?" Julia asked.

"Not at all. I'll have the twins stay and escort you back to the tavern to meet me for supper?"

Julia smiled. "I look forward to it."

The tavern was packed and loud with raucous, good-natured laughter once again. Elizabeth had been right, and

Shaw's supporters had cleared out fast. As Branna wended her way through the crowds, she greeted her own crew, well into their cups, and was thanked and congratulated by sailors, merchants, and evening ladies alike for ridding the port of the likes of Captain Shaw.

"May I buy you a drink, Captain?" Bridget was leaning against the bar, offering her a glass of rum.

"Thank you. It looks like this place is back to normal in no time."

"Thanks to you. And Julia."

The light was back in Bridget's eyes and the bruises fading. "I'm really glad you're all right, Bridget."

"Thank you, Branna. That means a lot. We owe you a great deal."

"No. You don't owe me anything at all."

Bridget looked past Branna's shoulder to the door and her face lit up. "I believe there's someone here for you, Captain."

Branna followed her gaze and her breath caught. Julia stood in the doorway, escorted by the twins. She was dressed in a flowing deep-blue dress with a tight bodice that flared out at her hips and cascaded down her legs. Her right arm was wrapped, and she limped, but it did nothing to diminish her breathtaking beauty.

"Thank you, gentlemen," Branna said to the twins, her eyes never leaving Julia. "I'll take it from here."

Branna let her gaze travel appreciatively along Julia's length. "You look…" She didn't have a word, so she slipped her hands around her waist and pulled her close, her lips pressing to Julia's in a kiss meant to convey every emotion.

Julia sighed, her left arm wrapping around Branna's neck to hold onto her.

Branna pulled away. "May I escort you to a table, Miss Farrow?"

"Thank you, Captain. That would be lovely."

She tucked Julia's good arm in the crook of her elbow. All eyes were on them as the crowd parted, this time Branna knew it was not for her but for Julia that folks moved aside out of respect and admiration. Branna's heart swelled with pride at the beautiful, courageous woman who chose to share her life. She held a chair for her.

They had been seated only long enough for the serving girl to pour them drinks when an older couple worked their way through the crowd to stand next to their table.

"Forgive the interruption," the man said. He had the sun-darkened and wind-worn look of a life spent at sea. He held the woman's hand tightly.

Julia raised her eyes and greeted them with a warm smile. "Good evening."

"Miss Farrow, I'm Captain Northcott. My wife and I own a small shipping fleet here in Port Royal. Work, among other things, had not been going well for us under Captain Shaw and we wanted, on behalf of all the merchants, to thank you most humbly for everything you've done to aid us."

"I'm pleased we could be of service, Captain."

Mrs. Northcott said, "We've heard at least some of what you went through, Miss Farrow, and we owe you a great debt."

"Anyone would have done the same."

"Not at all, my dear. Many able-bodied men had the opportunity to challenge Captain Shaw, and no one did. The courage and resilience you showed is beyond rival."

Julia flushed. "I don't know what to say."

Captain Northcott put his arm around his wife's shoulders. "We'll let you get back to your meal. We just wanted to say thank you and we would be honored, Miss Farrow, if we could call you a friend."

She extended her good hand. "The honor is mine, Captain."

The captain and his wife gripped Julia's hand in turn. "Good evening, Captain Kelly." The man nodded to Branna before he and his wife disappeared into the crowd.

Julia stared after them for a moment. "That was odd. I don't even know what to think."

Branna smiled. "I think, Miss Farrow, you've earned yourself quite the reputation."

CHAPTER SEVENTEEN

Upon arriving in Nassau, Genevieve and Merriam were waiting for them when Harris dropped Branna, Julia, Jack, Nat, and Gus at the dock before rowing back out for the other crew.

Branna grunted when Merriam shouldered her way past to fling her arms around Jack and kiss his face all over. She was stiff and the old wound in her belly ached fiercely.

"Take it easy, Mer." He gently pushed her away.

She glared at him and then Nat, who gave her a gap-toothed grin. "Jesus, what the 'ell happened to ya?"

"The same thing that happened here, I'd wager," Genevieve said dryly, looking Gus over with concern. The swelling in his face from his battle with Angus had gone down but the bruises were spectacular.

"I'm all right, Gen," he said, straightening to prove it.

"And you." Gen turned to Julia, taking in her wrapped arm, limp, and stitched head. "Should you even be on your feet?"

"I'll be fine with time," she said.

Merriam scowled at Branna. "How is it Kelly 'ere escaped without a scratch?"

"She didn't." Genevieve poked her gut and Branna flinched. "Sorry. Just checking."

Branna wrapped an arm around her middle. "Jesus, at least buy me a drink first."

"I'll buy you two," Genevieve said and took Gus's hand to lead them back to the courtyard.

A familiar figure was waiting for them at the entrance to Travers. Thomas Blythe straightened unsteadily from where he was leaning against the arch.

"Well, back from the wars again, eh, Kelly?" he slurred. "Been 'elpin' out some other poor bastards that ain't me?"

"Not now, Blythe," Gen snapped and pushed him aside so they could get past.

"Not ever, ya mean," he snarled and lunged toward Branna.

Branna wasn't so hurt she didn't see it coming and stopped him short with a hand fisted in his grimy shirt and the tip of her dagger beneath his chin. "You are testing my sympathy, Mr. Blythe."

Julia's hand gripped her arm. "Bran, leave him be. He's drunk."

"Piss off, whore!" he spat.

Branna leaned into his face, heedless of his sweat and booze stink. Blood trickled from the wound in his neck. "Say that again and see what happens."

"Captain," Jack said and stepped between them, forcing Branna and Thomas Blythe apart. "With your permission, I will kindly escort Mr. Blythe home."

"Aye, you best do that," she said. "Worry not, Mr. Blythe. You and I will finish this. You have my word."

Thomas Blythe spat a wad of phlegm in the dirt. "Your word ain't worth a bucket o' cold piss."

"So, what's your plan?" Genevieve asked Branna over supper after they had a chance to clean up and Branna was able to put Thomas Blythe out of her mind—again. He appeared to be a problem who was not going away, but Branna wasn't yet sure what she was going to do about it.

Nat and Gus were in fine fettle and had enjoyed telling of their latest adventure after a few drinks. Julia was quiet and withdrawn, lines of exhaustion and pain around her eyes, but she hung in there and recounted her story for Merriam and Genevieve.

"I think we're on land for a while," Branna said and sat back in her chair. She could feel Julia's gaze and knew what was coming.

"Branna, you just put the *Banshee* back in the water. You can't—"

"I can and I will. And it's not the *Banshee* that's staying. It's us. As in you and me. You need to heal, and as Genevieve so kindly demonstrated, I'm not at my best either. I think we could do with some more downtime."

Gus frowned. "I don't understand. What about the ship and the crew?"

Branna raised her brows at Gus and Nat. "That will be up to you, acting Captain Hawke. And, acting First Mate Hooper."

They stared at her, mouths agape, before breaking into enormous grins.

"Oh, Christ," Gen sighed.

"You're free to head back out as soon as the ship is restocked. I think it will be good for the crew to keep working together. The new men are still green, and I don't want to lose the momentum of this last sail. I can't imagine there's not a ship and captain out there not thinking to fill the void Captain Shaw left and I'd like our presence to continue to be felt."

"Branna, you don't have to stay. I'll be fine here with Genevieve and Merriam," Julia said.

Branna took Julia's hand. "No, we stay together. And I really could use a rest."

* * *

Despite Branna's constant reassurances Julia was troubled throughout the following week as Branna watched over the restocking of the ship and discussed with Gus and Nat their route, offered advice, and generally fretted about the ship going out without her. Blessedly, there had been no more run-ins with Thomas Blythe. Branna already seemed about to snap with the tension of remaining behind despite her constant assurances this was what she wanted.

Julia sat at the table in their room, periodically gazing out the window as the last of the boats came back in from the *Banshee*, while she finished writing a letter to her sisters, Alice and Kelly. The *Banshee*'s first order of business was to meet up with a merchant vessel heading north from Port Royal up the coast, to transfer a shipment of rum heading to Boston. The captain had agreed to pass the letter along to Julia's family while stopped in Charlestown.

She had much to tell them, leaving out the troubling details, and by the time she signed the letter with love her shoulder throbbed mightily. Her injuries were healing well but the damage to her shoulder had been extensive, and she worried she'd never wield a sword again—a concern that a few months ago, she never could have imagined.

Branna had tried to help by suggesting she start working on using her left hand, and they had agreed to start training again after the *Banshee* left port.

Julia replaced her sling, something she wore less often, and headed down to the docks to give Gus the letter. When she arrived, Merriam and Jack, and Gus and Genevieve were saying their goodbyes while Nat waited patiently. Branna looked on anxiously, and Julia felt the twinge of guilt again.

"Captain Hawke, fair winds," Branna said.

"We'll take good care of her." He and Nat stepped into the boat with Jack.

"Be safe," Julia said and handed Gus the letter.

He tucked it into his pocket. "See you soon."

Merriam and Genevieve made their way back down the dock. Julia joined Branna as she watched the boat row out to the ship and the crew made ready to sail. "Branna, you know you don't have to stay."

"Julia, I'll not have this conversation again. I want to. This is where I belong. With you."

"But—"

"Trust me, please."

She gave up. "I trust you. Are you coming up?"

"In a bit. I just want to see them off."

Julia wasn't sure she'd ever really believe Branna wouldn't rather be sailing. "Okay, I'll see you later."

Julia didn't feel like seeing Genevieve and Merriam just yet. She was feeling uncertain, and if she were honest, a little sorry for herself. She had gotten everything she wanted—Branna, a place on the crew, the respect of the men. But at what cost? She had killed a man and many others died because of her actions. She didn't yet know if she could live with the version of herself she would have to embrace to live a life with Branna. And she would never ask Branna to give up the life she had built.

At the end of the dock she turned away from Travers. A walk to collect herself and clear her head was in order. She jerked off the sling and jammed it into the pocket of her skirt.

She passed the repair yard, skirting around lumber, crates, and hardware. She caught a flash of orange tabby and smiled when Morrigan streaked by going after some vermin only she could see. Julia thought about calling to her, but Morrigan had made a new life for herself here and Julia didn't want to interrupt.

The repair yard was bustling at this time of the day. The air smelled of pine tar and fresh-cut wood and the sounds of woodworking. Men were moving back and forth between three small vessels undergoing repairs at the repair dock. As Julia walked past, fewer and fewer people were around this far away from port. She stopped at an old weather-worn building with a new sign—Lawford Shipwrights. She had never been down this far before.

There were wide double doors, closed and locked with a stout chain. Next to them a person-size door stood slightly ajar. For reasons she couldn't explain she pushed it open and entered.

It was dim with only a few lanterns burning around the large space, but it was enough to illuminate the object inside, a boat under construction, framed by a wooden scaffolding. The hull was smooth and polished, and Julia whistled softly as she ran her hand along the wood. It was too small to be a merchant vessel, perhaps only forty feet—a single masted sloop—and it was beautiful.

Julia walked around the small vessel, admiring her from all sides, the clean lines and well-crafted detail. This design was remarkable, like nothing she had ever seen before.

"May I 'elp ya, miss?"

Julia jumped. "I'm sorry. I didn't mean to intrude. The door was open and…" She trailed off as she took in the person to whom the voice belonged.

A young man, slightly built, with shaggy dark hair and dark eyes was wiping his tar-stained hands on a rag. "Ya lost, miss?"

"Hm, well, funny you should ask."

"Miss?"

"Never mind me. This boat is beautiful. Are the builders around? I'd love to speak with them."

"Yer lookin' at 'im."

"You? You built this?"

The young man winced. "Aye, miss."

"Forgive me. I hope I didn't offend you."

"I've 'eard it all before. An' worse. Kit Lawford." He extended his hand.

Julia shook it, grimacing slightly at the young man's strong grip against her injured shoulder. "Julia Farrow."

"Aye. I thought so."

"Have we met?"

"No, Miss, I've just…I've seen ya about. Yer the purser on the *Banshee* an' Capt'n Kelly's, um, yer her…I 'eard about what ya did in Port Royal."

"Yes," she said, not sure what else to say. The story was still fresh in everyone's mind and would be until something more interesting happened. She walked around the boat again and stopped at a well-lit table. On it were several large sheets of parchment, sketches and building plans carefully drawn to scale. "I've never seen anything like this."

"Nay, ya 'aven't. An' ya won't see this 'un either."

"But she's nearly finished."

"Aye, but wit' no buyer an' no coin, this is as finished as she's gonna get."

"I don't understand."

Kit reached under the table to a shelf and pulled out a bottle of rum and two glasses. "If ya like, miss, we can sit outside an' I'll tell ya."

Julia followed him out into the sunshine and Kit kicked over two crates for them to sit on before pouring each of them a glass of rum. In the daylight he looked even younger. "Forgive me for asking, Kit, but how old are you?"

He tossed back his glass then refilled it. "Twenty-two, miss, give or take a year."

"How did you learn to do all this?"

"My da an' three older brothers 'ave a building company in Port Royal. It's all I've ever known, but I 'ave ideas of my own. Thought my plans were cracked, they did, so I came 'ere."

Julia sipped her drink. "I understand that completely. It's hard living in someone else's shadow."

"Aye, miss. My da was fer it when I set out, 'cause he 'spects me ta come back an' he can gloat. Ta show 'is support he introduced me to a fancy bloke 'ere in Nassau. More coin than 'e knows what ta do with an' commissioned this sloop fer 'is son. He paid me fer the work an' I 'ad a couple o' boys from the repair yard ta help. We got this far."

"What happened?"

He laughed humorlessly. "The git son—beg yer pardon, miss—ran off ta Tortuga ta marry a girl. He's gone so there's no need fer the sloop. His da wasn't gonna pay me fer a boat 'e didn't need. No coin, no help, no boat."

Julia considered all he had said. "How much more do you have left to do?"

"Well, the next step is ta get 'er in the water an' get the mast up. The boys from the repair dock said they'd 'elp as soon as I get coin. After that, just the riggin', really. It's complex though. I've designed it ta be sailed wi' only two people. If they're skilled."

"Really? That's incredible. I'd love to see it."

"I can show ya the plans, miss."

"Would you accept my help? I have been injured recently and am unfit to sail with the *Banshee*. I find myself somewhat idle for a time."

Kit eyed her, skeptically. "I can't pay ya."

"It is I who will be paying you, Kit."

"Why would ya want ta do that?"

"Because I should know the rigging of my own boat, don't you think? And what better way to learn than to do the work myself."

"Beg yer pardon, miss. Are ya offerin' ta buy 'er?"

"Is she still for sale?" Between the money she had brought, her more-than-generous pay from her work on the *Banshee*, and her cut of the bounty from the *Ferryman*, Julia had more money than she knew what to do with. She also had time and couldn't think of a better way to spend it than learning to rig the boat she could call her own.

His eyes lit up. "Aye, miss."

"I'm not at my best at the moment, but I can assure you I work hard and—"

"Oy, miss, yer an officer on the *Banshee*. Ya got yerself a job—an' a boat."

"Excellent. I will come by this afternoon with an initial payment. And, Kit, you better call me Julia."

CHAPTER EIGHTEEN

Julia woke with a start, her heart pounding and muscles tense—as if she'd been running. Maybe she had been. Her nights had been restless since their battle with the *Ferryman*—she couldn't say his name, even in her own head. With everything that had happened in Port Royal and now the *Banshee* sailing without them, once again she felt uncertain about her path.

The first rays of sunshine were breaking over the horizon. Branna was curled against her back, an arm wrapped tightly around her and her face pressed into her neck, her slow breathing warm against her skin. Her love for Branna grounded her, still the one thing about which she wasn't uncertain.

She pushed aside her unease and made room for excitement at her new project. At working on something to call her own. Learning a new skill and making a new friend. Her spirit felt renewed, and she was anxious to start the day.

She had worked out a schedule with Kit. Branna would want to train in the mornings so she would meet at Kit's workshop in the afternoon. She still had not decided when to tell Branna.

She really wanted to keep it to herself for a while, but she didn't want Branna to think she was keeping secrets.

Branna's arm tightened around her, and she kissed the back of her neck. "You're awake early."

Julia's skin tingled at the feel of Branna's lips on her. "Just excited, I guess."

"Oh, aye?" Branna flattened her hand against Julia's naked belly and stroked her breasts. "Something I did?"

Julia laughed and turned in her arms to face her, wrapping her arms around her neck and pulling her in for a first kiss. "No, I was thinking about…" What if Branna didn't approve or thought she was being foolish? What if she was angry that Julia wanted her own boat, however small? Julia wanted this so much and wanted to believe Branna would be supportive, but she could be territorial, and it stopped Julia's tongue. "…just anxious to start training again."

"Really?"

"Yes. I've been feeling a little cooped up and frustrated. My foot has healed, and I really want to get back into shape." All of that was true.

Branna peered outside the window. It was early but light enough. "Well, we'll probably upset some folks with the noise this early, but we can get started if you want." She pulled Julia in for another long kiss, parting her lips with her tongue and exploring her mouth before pulling away. "Or, we could stay in bed another hour?"

"No." Julia swung out of bed. "I want to work out in the courtyard."

Branna sighed. "Okay."

"Draw your cutlass," Branna said as they stood facing each other in the middle of the courtyard. The tables were pushed out of the way to make room. Julia tried to hide it, but her discomfort was clear when she drew her blade from the scabbard and her shoulder hitched.

Branna frowned. "Extend your arm. Can you hold it up?"

Julia lifted her arm straight and within seconds was trembling from the strain. Her arm dropped to her side, her blade clattering to the stones as her fingers let go. "Bloody hell!"

Branna picked up Julia's weapon. "It's all right. It's just too soon." She unbuckled Julia's belt, slipping it from around her waist and removing the scabbard.

"No, Bran, I can do this."

"I know. Let's try this. Hold your arm tight to your body." Branna wrapped the leather belt around Julia's chest and right arm and buckled it in place. "This is what I would do to train someone in their nondominant hand anyway. How does that feel?"

Julia rolled her shoulder a little. "I'm okay."

Branna handed back her cutlass and Julia gripped it with her left hand. Branna drew a short sword with her left hand. She could use the practice, too. "Ready?"

Julia made the first move and caught her off guard, sending her stumbling back as their blades scraped together.

A moment later they nearly crashed into Merriam who staggered out of her room bleary-eyed and shouted over the clang of iron, "Don't ya 'ave anythin' better ta do?"

Julia held up a hand to pause Branna's next attack. "Sorry, Merri."

"I doubt it," Gen said as she came around from the bar with coffee and a plate of bread and fruit, placing it on a table far enough out of the way so it shouldn't be upended.

"Oy, Kelly, ya oughta shag more. That'll tire ya out," Merri suggested.

Gen snorted. "I assure you, Merriam, as someone who shares a wall, they need do nothing of the sort."

Branna reddened, but Julia laughed off the comment and charged her again.

They worked for nearly an hour. Branna had suggested they take a break several times, but Julia refused. She was flushed, clearly winded and visibly trembling, but she would not give up. Even Gen had expressed her concern, but her attention turned elsewhere when early morning customers arrived.

Branna didn't like this. Julia's eyes were bright and angry, and she was pushing herself too hard. She looked past Julia to see Thomas Blythe standing in the entryway, watching them. That man was not going away, but she couldn't worry about him at the moment. "Julia, we should stop."

"Not, yet," she panted, wiping sweat from her brow with the back of her arm. "I need to get better."

"You don't." Branna parried a blow and pushed her back. "I mean, there's time. Give yourself a chance to heal."

"No. I won't let him—"

"He's gone, Julia. You don't need to worry about him anymore."

Julia shook her head and came at Branna again, swinging erratically. "What about the next one? And the one after that?"

Branna grimaced, her belly aching at the strain as she parried three quick thrusts from Julia before she brought her sword down against Julia's cutlass, close to the hilt, knocking it from her hand with a clatter and driving her to her knees from the blow.

Julia grunted, her left hand going to the ground to stop herself from going all the way down.

"Julia! I'm sorry, are you hurt?"

"No," Julia replied breathlessly and sat on the ground, massaging her shoulder. "It's okay. I'm fine."

Branna knelt next to her and unbuckled the belt across Julia's arm. "What was that? Why wouldn't you stop? Are you—"

"I'm fine, Bran. I just tried to do too much."

Branna wasn't at all convinced that was true and wished Gen had been there to see what happened and maybe offer some insight. "Well, if it helps at all, you're moving really well, all things considered."

"Thanks. More tomorrow?"

"Are you sure?"

"I'm fine. I promise." Julia pulled damp hair off the back of her neck.

"You want to get cleaned up and go to the market with me for something to eat?" She hoped doing something that didn't involve mock life and death situations would get Julia to open up.

"Actually, I have somewhere to be."

"And I'm not invited? What are you up to?"

"Just something I'm working on." She leaned in and gave Branna a quick kiss before hurrying out of the courtyard.

Branna stared after her, confused and concerned. It was unlike Julia to be so noncommunicative. She was always the one sharing her ideas and feelings and pressing Branna to do the same.

"Where's she off ta so fast?" Merriam mumbled around a mouthful of food. "An' so sweaty."

"She wouldn't say."

"Oh. Julia 'as a secret." Merriam laughed.

Julia hurried to the docks, shaking free of her tension along the way. There was shouting, creaking wood and a tremendous splash long before she reached her destination. Excitement had her jogging the rest of the way to the waterline.

Her heart skipped when she saw the boat—her boat—bobbing in the water off the dock. Several large, smooth logs used to roll beneath the hull were scattered between the building and the water. There were a few men on the deck, and several more guiding the ship toward the dock with lines to her starboard gunwale. Kit was shouting orders as he paced up and down the dock, tending his own line as they pulled her in close and tied her off.

"She's in the water already?" Julia said.

"I know ya wanted ta be 'ere fer this, but the boys could 'elp either this mornin' or no' again fer a fortnight. I din figure ya fer the patient sort, miss."

"Please, call me Julia, and you figured correct, thank you." A line of men emerged from the shop with the mast carried on their shoulders. "They're doing the mast, too?"

"An' the shrouds. We wouldn't 'ave been able ta manage just the two of us. Do ya want ta watch or do ya want ta go over the plans?"

Julia was sore and tired—and hungry. She rather thought sitting down and going over plans would be more comfortable. "Let's go over the plans." She spied young master Henry, the boy she had befriended in the market, and a couple of other young boys hanging around watching the action. "Have you eaten? You mind if I send those boys for food?"

"I haven't, miss...er, Julia," Kit said.

Julia gave Henry enough coins to make his eyes bulge and the boys scampered off. Kit was staring at her curiously. "Something wrong?"

"Aye, um, beg yer pardon, but ya look a bit...do ya feel all right?"

Julia tucked the hair flying away behind her ear and looked down at her grimy, sweaty shirt. "Branna and I were training this morning and I came right over after."

"Cap'n Kelly didn't want ta come?"

"I haven't told her about this. And I would ask that you don't either, at least until I talk to her about it."

Kit busied himself dragging the drafting table outside the door to take advantage of the light. "Whatever ya want. Me an' the cap'n aren't friends."

"You've never met?" Julia asked and helped him with the table with her good arm.

"I know of 'er, 'course, but we've never spoken an' I doubt she's ever noticed me."

"Well, I very much look forward to introducing her to you. I'm sure she'll be as impressed with you as I am."

Kit unrolled the plans across the table, pinning them flat with drafting tools. He eyed Julia as she absentmindedly massaged her shoulder. "Were it yer shoulder ya injured?"

Julia pulled her right hand out of her pocket, finally. "Yes. It's been a slow recovery."

"Are ya all right ta do this? It's not easy work an' we can find someone—"

"I'll be fine. I want to learn and it's good for me to work it out. Should we get started?"

"Aye." Kit gestured to the plans. "She's forty feet with a mast height of forty-five feet. 'Er beam is thirteen feet an' she draws five. The sail area is seven hundred and forty-three square feet. The hull is cedar, built fer speed. It's lighter an' weathers better than other woods. The cabin 'as a clearance of just over six feet so ya shouldn't 'ave any problems. The deck an' interior is teak an' everything 'as been weatherproofed with my own personal recipe of tar an' plant wax."

They pored over the drawings for hours, Kit pointing out features and Julia asking questions about form and function. Some of it, she had to admit, was beyond even her experience. The rigging was advanced, way beyond what was currently out on the water, and she couldn't wait to learn to it.

"Oy, Kit. We're done," a worker called.

Kit waved to them and turned to Julia. "Ready ta see 'er?"

"Absolutely."

Julia ran her hand along the gunwales as she stepped carefully across the deck. There wasn't a nick or scratch on her and the wood smelled new. She was beautiful. She stood at the helm and ran her fingers over the glossy wood of the wheel, enjoying the feel of it under her hand.

"Ya won't get the full effect 'til she's fully rigged but this is one o' my ideas." Kit swung the boom aft, and it crossed within arm's reach of the helm.

Julia couldn't help but jump back slightly, her eyes going wide. "That's amazing."

"Aye. When she's rigged ya can tend the sails from the helm."

"Incredible."

"Ready ta go below?" he asked.

Julia followed him to the main hatch middeck. There were six steps down and the cabin opened into a small galley and lounge with bench seats and small port windows that opened. There was an alcove with a charting table on one side.

Through the galley a narrow corridor was lined with cupboards for storage and a head. The end of the corridor opened into a spacious cabin, a double bed taking much of the space. There were shelves, drawers, and more cupboards. The bed was large, almost as large as in their room at Travers and totally excessive for a boat this size.

Julia fought a smile. "Looks like we know where the young man's priorities lay."

Kit flushed. "The boy wanted ta...he asked that I..."

"It's lovely, Kit, and I wouldn't do anything different."

CHAPTER NINETEEN

The sun was setting by the time Julia made it back to Travers. Branna, Genevieve, and Merriam were in the courtyard having supper.

Branna rose when she saw her rush in. "Julia, where have you been? Are you okay?"

She gave Branna a quick peck on the lips. "I'm fine. I'm just going to run and get cleaned up and I'll be right down."

"Have you eaten?" Genevieve asked.

"No," Julia called over her shoulder as she headed up the stairs. "And I'm famished."

Julia hurriedly washed and changed into a skirt and blouse. She doubted very much she was going to be able to avoid telling Branna what she'd been up to. She admonished herself for even making such a big deal about it in her head. Of course, Branna would be supportive.

She headed back down feeling much more appropriately pulled together. Genevieve had the serving girls bring her a plate and she set to it as soon as she sat down. She could feel Branna's eyes on her.

"What worked up yer appetite?" Merriam asked.

Branna looked at Julia expectantly and even Genevieve seemed interested.

Julia's mouth was full, and she waved them off while she chewed. Before she had a chance to answer, a wet pile of wood clunked onto the table, spraying them with filthy water and knocking over glasses.

Branna surged out of her chair to draw her knife.

"Bloody 'ell," Merri screeched, her chair tipping over as she jumped back.

Thomas Blythe was unfazed at their reaction. He stood over them, wiping ocean slime from his hands onto his already soiled pants. "Oy, what's this then, Captain?"

"Blythe, I swear to all that is good and holy, I will run you through where you stand," Branna snarled.

"Steady, Branna." Gen scowled at the mess on the table. "Not in the courtyard. Take it outside."

Julia picked through the slimy pile of rotten wood and rope, wiping a thick layer of algae from the largest plank. A stamp on the wood was worn, but *Windswept* was legible. "What is this?"

Blythe sneered triumphantly. "Picked outta the rudder of a fishin' ketch. What's left of a rum cask—from the *Windswept*."

Branna snorted, her gaze flicking to the mess on the table. "Where?"

His confidence faltered. "Don't know where they picked it up."

Branna sheathed her knife. "This looks like it's been in the water as long as the ship has been missing. It could have come from anywhere. If you ask me, it's proof the *Windswept* is gone, not proof she's still out there."

"I ain't askin' ya, I'm tellin' ya and I'm goin' out ta find 'er."

"Thomas, don't be a fool," Gen said.

Branna barked a laugh. "Good, go. And take this mess with you."

"The mess is fer you."

"And you want me to do what with it, exactly?"

"Shove it up yer arse."

Branna wished she could relax in Julia's arms and go back to sleep. It was too early to get up, but her latest confrontation with Thomas Blythe had her on edge. Julia wasn't sleeping well either, and Branna was beginning to think her insistence that they stay behind and heal had been the most ridiculous idea she'd ever had. Neither one of them seemed to be doing particularly well—physically or emotionally.

Julia's arms tightened around her from behind. "Do you want to talk about it?"

"Thomas Blythe is haunting me, except he's not dead—but a living reminder of my shame," she blurted and gripped Julia's arms, pulling them together more tightly.

"Oh, Bran, don't think of it like that. Maybe this is an opportunity to set things right with Thomas. You couldn't help him then, but maybe you can help him now."

"How so?"

"He just wants what you have, Bran."

"Oh, aye? What's that?" Branna turned in Julia's arms.

"Closure."

"Aye, maybe. How do I give him that?"

Julia kissed her. "That I don't know."

"I thought you knew everything."

"I only pretend I do, but I know who really does."

"Who?"

"Gen. She'll know where to find him. Maybe he just wants to be heard and understood. Someone to believe him."

Branna headed down the dock to where Genevieve told her the *Billy Doon* was unloading their catch. Thomas Blythe had been working for them off and on. The dock was filling up with barrels of snapper, mackerel, and shrimp and the smell was powerful.

"Ahoy the boat!" she called out.

A sunburnt head popped out from around a stack of barrels on the deck. He was a wiry, shirtless young man with sun-bleached hair, in breeches too large. "Aye?"

"I'm looking for Thomas Blythe."

"'E in trouble?"

"No. Just need a word with him, please."

"Who's askin'?"

She wasn't surprised he didn't recognize her. She wasn't familiar with his boat either. They were new to the area as many ships were in the absence of Cyrus Jagger. "Let him know Branna Kelly would like a moment of his time."

The boy's eyes went wide. He may not have recognized her, but he knew who she was. "Right away, Cap'n."

The young man disappeared below and did not return. Instead, Thomas Blythe shot up from the hatch as if being pushed from below.

"Oy, bugger off, mate!" Blythe took a swipe at someone below him, and Branna imagined the other man crouched within earshot but out of sight.

"Mr. Blythe," Branna said from the dock.

His head whipped toward her, and he staggered, reaching for a barrel to right himself. He was drunk. "'Ope ya didn't come fer an apology."

"Came to offer one."

"Fer what?"

"For not doing more to help when the *Windswept* went missing."

"Ya didn't do a bloody thing ta help."

Branna held out her hands in what she hoped was a placating gesture. He was right. When the *Windswept* went missing she had been too wrapped up in her own cause and her own anger to spare the time for him. "I know, and I'm sorry."

"A little late fer that ain't it, Cap'n? I came ta ya last year 'cause I trusted ya. Ya 'ad the best ship, the best crew, the most coin, an' I thought ya would understand..." His voice hitched with despair.

"I *do* understand."

His expression went from desperate to enraged. "But ya turned yer back."

Shame tightened her chest. She remembered. He had pleaded for her help in searching for his brother and she had mocked him and sent him away. She vowed nothing would come between her and her vengeance. "I'm here now."

He laughed bitterly. "If yer lookin' fer forgiveness, Cap'n, ya came ta the wrong place."

"You're going after her in this?" She gestured to the small fishing vessel not designed for the open ocean for long periods of time.

"Someone 'as ta."

"I can help."

"Oh, aye? With what ship?"

Her jaw clenched. There really wasn't much she could do. "When the *Banshee* returns."

"Too late fer that. Do yer penance somewhere else."

Julia took the grilled skewers of chicken from Henry and gave him and his friends a coin. She handed a skewer to Kit and they lowered themselves onto a large crate on the dock to eat.

With some unexpected help from Henry and the pack of boys from the market, whose numbers had grown over the days, they had nearly completed the rigging. Julia had treated them all to lunch in thanks.

"So, what do ya think?" he asked around a mouthful.

Julia sighed happily as she gazed at the vessel. "There are no words."

"What are ya gonna call 'er?"

"I've been thinking about that. I've had a few ideas. Maybe something to honor my family or the *Firelight*. The ship that was…that I was…"

"Aye, Julia, I know yer story."

Julia sucked in a steadying breath. "But nothing has felt right. The entire reason I even wanted any of this was because I need something independent of my life with Branna—something just for me. But when I think about who I've come to be, how I've grown and changed and what's meaningful to me now, I owe that to finding Branna again, making things right with her, discovering our love for the first time—again. That sounds confusing even to me."

Kit stared out to sea. "Like the firebird risin' from the ashes?"

"Exactly. This boat is symbolic of a new beginning for me."

"How's yer Latin?"

"Not as good as my mother would have liked. Why, how's yours?"

"It's shite—beg yer pardon. But I know the word fer *dawn*."

"Aurora," Julia murmured. "Also, the name for the Northern Lights. I love it."

"Aye. Shall that be 'er name, then?"

Julia laughed and threw her arms around Kit. "I am so blessed to have found you. You are a treasure. I can't wait for Branna to meet you and see your work."

CHAPTER TWENTY

The walk back to Travers seemed to take an eternity. Branna hadn't expected the meeting with Thomas Blythe to go well, but she hadn't counted on feeling worse. Regret and shame weighed heavily, and all she wanted to do was fall into Julia's arms and unburden herself. She needed forgiveness, but she didn't know from whom.

Travers was the usual midday busy. Genevieve was behind the bar and gave her a nod of greeting. Merriam was bustling about entertaining groups of men, bringing drinks, batting her lashes and regaling them with stories.

Branna grabbed for her as she flitted by. "Is Julia around?"

Merriam whirled, carefully balancing the tray of ales. "She left right after ya this mornin'. Ya look like arse, by the way."

"Do you know where she went?"

"I ain't 'er mum. But I saw her headin' ta the repair docks."

Branna unclenched her jaw and relaxed her hands. Merriam was just being Merriam and she wasn't known for her sensitivity—especially when it came Branna.

"Where are you off to in such a sulk without telling me how things went with Thomas Blythe?" Genevieve asked as she hurried to catch up with her.

Branna was trudging along toward the repair docks. She slowed as she spied Morrigan and crouched down, clucking her tongue to get the cat's attention. "I'm not sulking."

Morrigan glared at the interruption before her tail flicked in recognition and she padded silently over to Branna, winding in and out of her legs. She purred loudly and arched her back under Branna's scratching fingertips. "You still love me don't you, girl?"

"Says the woman pleading for affection from a yard cat."

"Why are you following me?" Branna watched Morrigan scoot back to her business between the crates.

"You have a look about you."

Branna's eyes narrowed. "What look?"

Gen jabbed a finger in her face. "That look. Like you'd rather be stabbing something."

"I'm just looking for Julia."

"Mind if I accompany you?"

"I don't need help, Genevieve." Julia's laugh drifted to them from nearby. "See? Found her."

They rounded barrels of tar and coiled line. Julia sat on a crate by the dock with her arm around a young man. Branna blinked, her mouth dropping open when Julia leaned into him, laughing and speaking animatedly.

"So, we did," Genevieve said.

Branna tore her gaze away and stepped back around the barrels so she couldn't be seen, her fingernails digging into her palms.

"I suppose now is as good a time as any to discover what Julia has been up to," Gen said.

"I don't need the bloody details." Branna started back but was pulled up short by Gen's strong grip on her wrist.

"Branna Doireann Colleen Kelly. Over my dead body will I allow you to stomp off and brood yourself into a froth over Julia—who loves you beyond what is sensible—doing nothing but spending time with someone with whom you are not familiar."

"Did you just channel my mother?"

"Bite your tongue." Genevieve stepped out from behind the barrels.

"No, Gen, don't!" Branna hissed. She lunged for her and missed. Branna pressed her back into the crates, out of sight. What was wrong with her? She was acting the fool.

"Julia, there you are," Genevieve called.

"Gen? What are you doing here?"

"Captain Kelly and I were looking for you, in fact."

"Branna's here? Where?"

"Bollocks," Branna hissed, going rigid. She squeezed her eyes shut and exhaled slowly before stepping out into view. Julia and the unfamiliar young man were holding half-eaten skewers and wearing matching expressions of confusion. "Here. I was just, um, I saw Morrigan and was…"

Julia smiled. "I was just talking about you. I'm glad you're here. There's someone I'd like you to meet."

"Awfully bold," Branna muttered.

"Branna Kelly, this is Kit Lawford," Julia said, her smile faltering after a beat of Branna's silence.

"Ah, of Lawford Shipwrights fame," Genevieve said. "I've heard good things about you, Mr. Lawford. I'm Genevieve Travers."

"Thank ya fer sayin' so." He gave her a little bow. "It's a pleasure ta meet ya, ma'am."

"Ma'am?" Genevieve gasped theatrically. "I take it all back."

Kit reddened. "Beg yer pardon ma…er…miss."

"Genevieve is fine, Mr. Lawford," she said, extending her hand.

He shook it. "Call me Kit."

Branna kicked a stone harder than she intended and it smacked into a crate with a loud bang.

"Branna, are you all right?" Julia asked.

"Aye, never better."

"Then why are you behaving this way?"

"Is there something you want to tell me, Julia?" Branna's gaze flicked between her and Kit Lawford.

Julia brightened. "Yes. I've been wanting to tell you all week. It was such an odd meeting, but Kit and I have been—"

"No!" Branna shouted.

"—finishing a boat for me." Julia frowned. "What is wrong with you?"

Branna blinked at her. "Sorry. What did you say?"

Julia pointed to the docks. "I bought a boat."

Branna looked at the gleaming new little sloop tied up at the dock. "You bought a boat?"

Genevieve smothered a laugh with her hand. "And what a beautiful boat it is. I see your work is as excellent as people say, Kit."

"Folks say that?" Kit gaped at her.

"Not yet." Genevieve put her arm around him and steered him back toward the tavern. "Come with me and we'll get that rumor started."

Julia stared at her. "You look so confused, Bran. What did you think I was going to say?"

Branna shook her head and inhaled deeply. "Nothing, I just...it was foolish."

"Please, tell me you did not think I was entertaining the affections of another." Julia cupped Branna's face in hands and pinned her with her gaze.

Branna's throat tightened and the heat of shame crept up her face. "Like I said, foolish."

Julia's mouth pressed into a hard line, and she nodded slowly. "Have I not been clear enough about what I want, Bran?"

Branna shrugged. "You said you wanted something for yourself."

"A boat of my own, not another lover! Honestly, after everything we've been through, how could you think that?"

"I'm sorry, Julia. You've been disappearing all day and not telling me what you were doing. I had a bad morning and I saw you together and I just...I'm sorry."

"You're right. I was being secretive about it. I wasn't sure if you would be supportive, and I just wanted to keep it to myself—"

"Wait. When have I not been supportive of you?"

Julia winced. "Never. I know. I should never have thought that. I guess, maybe, after Port Royal, I've been feeling a little uncertain."

"Uncertain of me?"

"No, Bran. Uncertain of me. Uncertain of this new me that I'm so unfamiliar with."

Branna wrapped her arms around Julia's waist and pulled her close. "You'll tell me if there's something I can do to help, right? No more secrets from you?"

"And no more doubts from you?"

"Aye, I'll never doubt you, again." Branna kissed her.

Julia grinned. "There is something you can do, then."

"Anything."

"Sail with me, Branna Kelly. Be my first mate."

* * *

Julia checked their course. Though they were out of sight of Nassau she was familiar enough with these waters to know in another day they would be within sight of the islands to which they were headed, uninhabited and unnamed, but popular for fishing and foraging with pristine beaches, fresh water, and lush foliage and fruit. They could take their time, circle the islands and then head back to Nassau. A proper holiday and a chance to reconnect with each other.

Satisfied with their heading, she settled back down on the deck, the wood warm beneath her, and waited for Branna who emerged with two plates of fresh fruit, cheese, bread, and dried meat. She had mugs of ale balanced precariously on the plates.

"Thank you. Gen spared no expense getting us stocked it seems," Julia said, taking a plate.

"As excited as you were to get out on the water to try out the *Aurora*, she was that excited for me to get out of her hair and stop 'sulking about' as she put it." Branna settled on the deck next to her.

"Aren't you going to ask where we're headed?" Julia asked.

"You're the captain. I trust you."

"Are you happy to be back out on the ocean?"

"I'm always happy to be on the ocean. And I'm positively delighted for someone else to be in charge."

"Not worried I'll run us aground?"

"It's your boat. Do with her what you will."

"Well, while we're eating, will you talk to me about something?"

"Anything."

"Tell me about Thomas Blythe. I know it's been weighing heavily on you."

Branna scooted over to lean her back against the port gunwale and get into a little bit of shade. She propped her hands on her knees. "You already know the story of the *Windswept*."

"I do. Now I want to know the rest."

"Not much to tell. A few weeks after she went missing, maybe a month, I don't remember…Several ships had reported back to port that there had been no sign of her. No wreckage, no crew turned up and no one claimed responsibility for sinking her. There had been no storms. The *Banshee* came back into port for restock and Thomas Blythe found me. He asked for my help. He *begged* for my help."

"And you said no."

"And I said no. Because nothing or no one was as important as finding the *Serpent's Mistress*. Because no one else's pain could touch mine. No one could possibly understand loss like I did. It would have cost me nothing to help Thomas Blythe and I couldn't be bothered."

"Have you thought of talking to him? Maybe you could—"

"That's where I was before I came looking for you the other day. When I saw you with Kit and I thought…"

"Oh. It didn't go well, I assume."

"It did not."

"Branna, we all have moments from our past we wish we could change. We all live with regret." Julia reached for her hand. "Anyone who says otherwise is either lying or living an unexamined life."

A grim smile tugged at the corner of Branna's mouth.

"I agree, your past may be darker than most. But you *chose* that path."

"I prefer to think the path chose me."

"You had no control over what happened to you and what happened to your family. But you chose the path of vengeance. You did that and you got exactly what you wanted. You made your decisions and now you must live with that. I understand it's painful for you, and I have no doubt there are many things you wish you could take back or do differently. Perhaps there are some that you can. And I hope you know you never have to do it alone. I will be with you and help in any way I can."

"I know. Thank you, machree."

Julia put an arm around her and pulled her close. "You're not nearly as hard to love as you think you are. And the things you've done are not nearly as shameful as you think—the ones I know about, anyway."

Branna took a shuddering breath and relaxed into Julia's arms, holding her tightly.

They sat like that for several minutes until Julia noticed the quiet and looked up to see the mainsail hanging limp and unmoving against the mast. The air was perfectly still.

What's wrong?" Branna asked.

"Dead calm."

CHAPTER TWENTY-ONE

The water was like glass and there wasn't a ship or land in sight. They hadn't been talking long, but Julia didn't know when the wind had died or if they'd drifted at all. She checked the compass. They were still pointed the way she had intended. They just weren't moving. She lowered the mainsail so they wouldn't be caught unaware if the wind surged.

Julia stood, hands on hips. "I need a spyglass."

Branna disappeared below and returned with the old but perfectly functional instrument she had purchased in the market for the trip.

Julia held it to her eye and shook her head. They were too far out from anywhere to sight land. She hadn't, until now, felt the need to chart their position, but with no wind, no way to power themselves and no land in sight, it would be irresponsible not to mark their last known position in case they drifted.

"We need the charts."

"In the galley." Branna took the spyglass and gazed around while Julia went below to mark their course.

"So what now?" Branna asked when she returned.

Julia looked out over the smooth crystal water. There was nothing they could do now so they might as well enjoy themselves. She unbuttoned her blouse and dropped it to the deck. "I have an idea."

Branna's brows rose. "Oh?"

Julia quickly kicked off her boots and shimmied out of her skirt, letting everything fall to a pile on the deck. She stepped up to the gunwale and dove into the sea.

When she surfaced, she grinned at Branna and slicked her hair back "Are you coming or not?"

Branna stripped out of her clothes and kicked the rope ladder over the side before diving in. She slipped her arms around Julia's waist, pressing their naked bodies together, their lips mere inches apart.

"Mmm," Julia hummed and laced her fingers behind Branna's neck, spinning them in a lazy circle. "I love you, Captain Kelly."

"That's First Mate Kelly to you." Branna pulled Julia close, kicking her legs to keep them both afloat, and crushed her mouth to Julia's.

Julia groaned into the kiss, forgetting to tread water and sinking immediately, pulling Branna down with her. They came up laughing and spluttering. Julia threw her arms around Branna's neck. "Take me to bed."

There was a trail of water from the deck, through the galley and down the corridor to the sleeping cabin as they clutched and grappled with each other before finally crashing onto the bed.

Branna rolled atop Julia and descended on her, devouring her mouth before kissing behind her ear, down her neck and across her breasts.

Julia arched under her, raking her hands across her back, marking her with her nails. She groaned when Branna turned her attention to her breasts, nipping and sucking one with lips and teeth while kneading the other with a strong hand.

Branna's hands stroked Julia's body, finding the hot wetness between her legs. Julia gasped as Branna parted her and plunged inside.

She cried out, her nails digging into Branna's shoulders and her hips bucking against Branna's hand as her orgasm built unbearably fast before exploding through her body.

Branna slowed her thrusts but didn't withdraw, curling her fingers against the inside of Julia's contracting walls. Julia trembled and her muscles spasmed around Branna's hand as she continued to stimulate her.

Another climax built slower and hotter, her belly tightening. She wrapped her legs around Branna's waist, tilting her hips and pulling Branna deeper. She was nothing but pure pleasure and her vision blurred to spots of light until she peaked with a shout of Branna's name.

Branna cracked her eyes and the cabin swam into view. She was hot with Julia draped across her, still sleeping deeply. The room smelled of salt air and sex and she felt loose and tremendously sated, Julia's weight comforting and warm.

She had no idea how long they had made love nor how long she had slept. She didn't think it had been through the night, but she felt rested and alert. The boat was rocking gently, the wind apparently having picked back up. She slipped out from beneath Julia, careful not to disturb her, though she suspected nothing short of cannon fire could manage that.

There was a basin of fresh water and Branna scrubbed her skin of salt water, sweat and sex before dressing in clean clothes and braiding her hair. Julia hadn't moved and Branna placed a gentle kiss across her lips before moving to the galley and preparing herself a meal of dried meat and bread.

Though they wouldn't sail again until Julia was ready—it was her boat after all—Branna figured she could chart their new location. Hopefully, they hadn't drifted too far. She stepped up to the deck, her mouth dropping open.

The air was damp and heavy with fog so thick Branna could barely make out the helm from where she stood. She could see nothing beyond the gunwales on either side. The mast disappeared into the fog only a few feet above her head. "Bloody hell." Her voice sounded muted, absorbed into the heavy air.

It was gloomy—but not completely dark—and so disorienting Branna had no sense if it was dusk or dawn. She stood still, feeling the slow rocking of the sloop. The wind had picked up slightly, enough to drift them but not enough to power them. Without any sense of direction, though, they would have no way to know where they were or which way to go. They would have to wait until the fog lifted.

There was movement below. "Julia, you need to see this."

Julia's head popped up from the stairs, mouth full of whatever she was snacking on. She swallowed hard. She held out her hand, grasping at the air, the fog so thick you could feel it. She repeated Branna's moves exactly, spinning around and looking up. "Oh, my God. This is…I've never seen anything like this."

Branna crossed the deck to the helm. She would feel less disoriented if she knew what direction they were facing. She wiped off the glass face of the compass with her sleeve and frowned.

"What's wrong?" Julia asked.

"I don't know." She tapped on the glass. "Something's wrong with it."

The needle spun wildly, first in one direction and then the other, then back and forth, erratically.

"What do we do?" Julia asked.

"There's nothing we can do. Even if we knew where we were, we can't see and there's not enough wind to get us anywhere."

Julia frowned. "I don't like this."

"Everything's fine. The sloop is stocked for days. We just need to wait for the fog to clear and we're on our way. Until then"—Branna kissed her and pulled her close—"I can think of something to keep us busy."

"Are you kidding? I can barely walk as it is."

"Who said anything about walking?"

"Stop." Julia turned her head sharply.

Branna froze. "What's wron—"

"Shh. Do you hear that?" Julia whispered, staring into the fog.

Branna pulled away and cocked her head, following Julia's gaze though she could see nothing. She could hear it. A deep, bone-chilling groan of wood. "What the hell?"

"Branna, what is that?"

"I don't know." She searched frantically for any clue what was out there. The water was lapping hard at the hull and the sloop began to rock. "It's big and it's close."

Branna's heart hammered in her chest. There was no way they could be seen. She searched the deck, grabbing up a fishing gaff. It was only six feet long, but it was all she had.

"Look out!" Julia screamed.

Branna whirled to see the dark looming shape of a ship's bow split the fog a few yards from the port side. It wasn't moving fast but the ship was easily the size of the *Banshee*. "Christ! Julia, hold on!"

Julia was thrown to the deck and somehow Branna was able to keep her footing and jam the gaff into the hull. Her hands slid painfully along the pole as she struggled to fend off the ship and move the sloop out of its path. The ship groaned and the sloop rocked against the opposing forces.

Branna stared up at the prow, almost losing her footing when she saw the figurehead, weatherworn and rotting but unmistakably familiar. She redoubled her efforts as she felt Julia come up behind her and add her strength to the gaff pole.

Together they pushed the sloop out of the way and the ship creaked past, scraping along the hull of the *Aurora*, gouging the wood and cracking a portion of the gunwale. The ship drifted past and they stood watching it slowly disappear into the fog.

Branna snapped out of her daze and ran to the jib, quickly raising it to gather what little wind there was.

"Branna, what are you doing?"

"Going after her," Branna said as the jib filled. She kept her eye on their last known position as she moved to the helm and changed their course to follow the ship.

"What! Why? They couldn't see us, we can't see them, they're clearly out of their minds for even trying to sail in this fog."

Branna was silent for a long time, peering hard into the fog for some sign of the ship. "I know that ship."

"And? What ship is it?"

"It's the *Windswept*."

CHAPTER TWENTY-TWO

"You're not serious," Julia said. "How can you even be sure? We can barely see through this fog."

Branna's gaze flicked to her briefly before concentrating again on the fog. "I recognized the figurehead. A bust of a naked woman, her hair blown back from her face."

"Bran—"

"Julia. Maybe I'm wrong but I need to know. Are you going to help me?"

"Of course, I am. What do you want me to do?"

"Take the wheel." Branna reclaimed the gaff pole and moved to the bow.

"Do you think we should raise the main? Get some more speed?"

Branna shook her head but didn't turn around. "They were big and slow in this weak wind. I don't want to overshoot them."

Julia relaxed her eyes, looking for subtle shadows, shimmers in the haze or disturbances in the water. There, ahead off the port side, she caught a glimpse of movement.

"Branna." She lowered her voice, unsure why she felt the need to whisper. She waited for Branna to turn and nodded in the direction of the dark, wavering shape as she adjusted course to head toward it.

Branna's hands were tense around the gaff as they waited for the sloop to come alongside the ship. Julia could hear her now, the wood creaking and groaning against the soft motion of the sea. She strained to hear anything else, footsteps or voices. It was quiet but for the gentle lapping of the sea and the creak and scrape of the hulls.

Julia worked to keep the sloop alongside her, close but not crashing into her. They'd suffered enough damage already and they were damn lucky they weren't taking on water after that collision. Kit was going to have a fit.

Branna paced the length of the sloop, eyeing the hull and looking for any way up. She was intact but weatherworn and the barnacles were extensive. Routine maintenance had obviously not been part of her last year.

Up near the bow there was a loop of line dangling over the side and Branna lunged for it with the gaff. Once. Twice. The third time she jumped up on the gunwale and clung with one arm to the shroud to extend as far as she could. She snagged the line with the hook and jerked it. It snaked down, unraveling and showering her with cockroaches.

"Jesus!" Branna jumped and shook a few off her clothes and crushed them under her boot. She crushed one more as it skittered across the deck. "Sorry."

"Are you all right?"

"Aye." Branna wrapped her arm around the line, tugging mightily. It seemed strong enough. She tied off the free end to a cleat on the deck of the sloop.

"Will that hold?" Julia asked as she lowered the jib and stowed the sail.

"Aye, it should." Branna stood with her hands on her hips, staring up at the ship.

"Now what?" Julia stood next to her.

Branna tugged on the line again. "I'm going over."

Julia eyed the rope and rolled her shoulder, sore from her hard fall onto the deck. "Branna, I can't climb that."

"Good. Because you're staying here."

"Like hell I am. We do this together, remember?"

"Julia, I don't think you should—"

"Branna. We can't have this both ways. We either trust and support each other or we don't. We both go or no one does, understand?"

"Okay, you're right. You're right."

Julia sighed. "I usually am."

"I'll be back in a minute." She went below.

Julia wrapped her arms around herself. She felt chilled, though the air was warm. The fog had not moved at all, and she could barely see the gunwales of the ship, and she could see neither the bow or the stern. It was eerie and unsettling, making the ship seem much larger than it was.

Despite Branna's certainty Julia wasn't ready to believe this was the *Windswept*, though the ship did seem to be adrift. The crew could be there. They could be hurt or sick or... Julia didn't want to think about what else. The quiet was maddening.

"Hello?" she called. "Ahoy the ship! Can anyone hear me?"

"I can hear you," Branna said as she came up from below, carrying both their blades, a lantern and a satchel of supplies. "What are you doing?"

"I just thought we should announce ourselves before we board."

"There's no one there." She handed Julia her scabbard and cutlass. "Put this on."

"If you don't think anyone is on board, why do we need to be armed?" she asked as she buckled on her weapon.

Branna slung her own sword across her back. "I could be wrong. I'm going up. I'll find a ladder for you." She swung over the gunwale and onto the rope before Julia had a chance to respond.

Julia gripped the rope, keeping it taut as Branna shimmied up, arms and legs wrapped tightly around the line and inching her along. She wrapped her arms over the gunwale and scrabbled her feet against the hull, hauling herself over onto the deck with a grunt.

Branna dropped onto the deck, panting from exertion and a deep ache in her side. Sweat trickled down her face and neck.

"Bran?" Julia called from below.

Branna pushed herself to her feet and gave Julia a wave. "I'm good." She looked at Julia, hazy through the fog, and realized she could keep her safe by simply not helping her over.

"Don't even think about it, Branna."

"Right. I'll just look around for something." She scanned the deck, the fog so heavy she could only see a few yards in front of her. The deck was in shambles. Loose, rotting lines, overturned and broken crates and barrels, broken tools and shredded sails. She could hear the flapping sails in the low breeze. If she strained her eyes, she could make out the pale motion of the sails smacking against the mast.

If there was a ladder it would be near the gunwale. She moved along the starboard side, kicking refuse and broken wood out of the way. She heard the scuttling of rodents and insects and suppressed a shudder as she upended their homes, sending them racing for cover.

She had just about decided to move across the deck to the other side to search when she pulled some crates away from the side and caught sight of a length of rope ladder. She hefted it and guessed there was about ten feet. It was plenty long enough but a few of the rungs were cracked or outright broken. They'd likely not support Julia's weight.

"Branna?"

Branna wasn't happy about it, but she needed to let her try. "Hold on. I've got it."

She laid the hooked end over the gunwale and dropped the ladder over the side nearest to where Julia was standing. "Wait a minute." She held up her hand to stop her as Julia moved to climb the gunwale. "I'm going to come down first. Hand me up the lantern and supplies."

She descended slowly, skipping the questionable rungs, until she could reach out to take the lantern and satchel from Julia. She climbed back up as fast as she dared. "Don't step on the third and seventh rung."

It was a tense few minutes while Julia climbed. Branna helped her over the gunwale and Julia rolled her shoulder.

"All right?" Branna asked.

Julia nodded and took a deep breath, her gaze sweeping over what little of the deck she could see. "Should we work our way aft?"

"Aye." Branna shouldered the satchel and picked up the lantern and led the way to the quarterdeck.

They walked quietly, though there seemed to be no one to hear them. The deck was in shambles the entire way and nearing the main mast revealed a single somewhat-intact sail which was what propelled the ship. What was left of the rest of them were either stowed or hung in tatters, flapping uselessly.

Branna paused outside the captain's quarters, the logical place to start, and lit the lantern. She pushed the door open and entered first, Julia following closely behind.

The lantern cast a dim glow as the persistent thick fog penetrated even the closed quarters. More scuttling could be heard as rats and roaches and whatever other manner of infestation skittered away from the light.

Julia gave a small cough, her hand covering her face. "Dear, God."

Branna swallowed and cleared her throat at the unmistakable odor of death. She held the lantern high and moved farther into the room. It had been destroyed. The navigation table was overturned, charts ripped to shreds and partially eaten by rats and insects. Instruments were broken and bent, some sticking out of the walls. Books and papers lay scattered about the floor with clothes and other items they couldn't identify.

Branna gripped Julia's arm, guiding her around broken glass on the floor, the windows smashed out. She swung the lantern around and moved to the bed. The bedding was tangled and dragging on the floor. There were thick, dark stains all over the bedsheets, wall, and floor. Though old, the smell was stronger as they stood over the source—congealed blood, vomit, and all other manner of sick, moldering body fluids.

Julia gasped. "Oh, God, what happened here?"

Branna pulled Julia away from the bed and soiled linens. She focused on the room and began to kick through the pages, charts and books on the floor.

"What are you looking for?" Julia asked, peering around at the mess on the floor.

Branna squatted down and flipped through a stack of books, pulling out a thick, leatherbound volume. "This."

"The ship's log," Julia said and moved toward the aft windows. "Branna, look."

Branna followed Julia's gaze to a carved wooden plank on the wall with one word. *Windswept.*

Branna jammed the book into the satchel and held her hand out for Julia. "Come on. Let's get out of here."

They stepped back out onto the deck to see there had been no change in the fog. In fact, it appeared heavier than ever.

Julia raked her hands through her hair and blew out a frustrated breath. "Do we check the rest of the ship? See if any of the crew are—"

"There's no one here. Whatever happened here happened a long time ago and we can barely see a thing. I say we wait for the weather to clear. We can't go anywhere until then anyway. I don't like moving around this ship partially blind, there could be damage we don't know about. In the meantime, we can look at the log and maybe find out something more."

Julia visibly relaxed at Branna's decision. "Fine with me. Let's get the hell—"

A distinct thump vibrated the deck beneath their feet stopping Julia's words and her hand flew to her chest. "What?"

"It was probably just some cargo tipping over," Branna said.

"There could be someone here, Branna."

"We'll come back when the weather clears." She did not like this at all and her skin prickled in warning.

"They could need help."

Branna pressed her lips together in a thin line. She knew Julia was right and she wanted—needed—to do right by this ship, but she had a very bad feeling about this. "We stay together, okay?"

"Agreed."

CHAPTER TWENTY-THREE

"We're going to need more light." Branna handed Julia the lantern before heading back to the captain's quarters. "Wait here."

"I thought we were staying together," Julia hissed, holding up the light, but Branna had disappeared into the fog. She turned in a slow circle, surveying the deck for any signs of life. She heard nothing save for the creaking of the ship, flap of ragged sails, and soft lapping of water.

A heavy, muffled thump came from somewhere to her right and Julia spun in the direction she thought it originated, her heart hammering in her chest. "Branna?"

A hand came down on her shoulder and Julia shrieked and spun around.

"Whoa! It's just me."

"Bloody hell!" Julia gasped, a hand going to her chest.

"Are you all right?"

"I thought I heard something."

"Let's see if this will light." Branna held up a small lantern and gave it a little shake to hear the small amount of oil sloshing around. She set the lanterns on the deck and searched the satchel for the pouch of dry tinder. She lit the tinder from the working lamp and touched the flame to the wick. It caught after a moment and a weak flame grew. Branna handed the small lantern to Julia.

Julia scowled at the pitiful light. "Thanks."

"What? I'm going first and need the better light." She shouldered the satchel and reached for Julia's hand.

The *Windswept* was similar in design to the *Banshee* and Julia was relieved Branna seemed to have no trouble finding her way around. They crossed the deck and made it to the hatch to go below without incident despite the limited visibility.

Branna tested each step carefully as she climbed slowly down. The dark was nearly absolute, and their lanterns lit only a small radius of space around them. The air was heavy and dank, smelling of rotting wood, mold, animal droppings, and the fetid odor of death.

"Stay close," Branna whispered at the base of the steps before she moved off down the narrow corridor.

The door to the first room was ajar and Branna toed it open and leaned in. They were assaulted with a hot rush of rank air, and she coughed, covering her mouth. She held the lantern high and stepped into the small quarters, the light illuminating the grotesque dark stains across the deck and bulkheads. There was little else to see.

They peered in the next few cabins with the same result. The farther they explored the depths of the ship, the heavier and more stagnant the air. They crept along silently, speaking only to warn each other of obstacles or hazards in their path.

The next cabin was a horror. Julia could only assume someone had died in there from the amount of blood and stench. Julia's skin crawled when the lantern's light sent vermin skittering back into the shadows.

"What killed these men?" Julia whispered. Sweat from the heat and tension trickled down the back of her neck. "And where are the bodies?"

Branna seemed just as unsettled at the sinister circumstances. "It looks like they were killed in their bunks. The galley should be next. Come on."

Branna led them down the corridor and a subtle change in the air, the cloying stench loosening its grip, told them the space was opening up into a larger room. She quickened her pace and Julia was close behind her when the deck gave slightly beneath her boot with a sharp crack.

Branna froze when the deck cracked again. She spun and shoved Julia hard in the chest as the wood splintered beneath them. "Get back!"

Julia staggered back but managed to keep her feet as she crashed into the bulkhead in the narrow corridor and a section of the corridor floor disintegrated, taking Branna and the light with it. "Branna!"

Julia gripped her weak lantern and dropped to her hands and knees to distribute her weight, crawling as near as she dared across the deck. There was light below, but she couldn't see her. "Branna! Bran, say something."

The wood was weakening the closer she got to the edge, and she was in danger of going through herself. She needed to get back to the stairs and get down to the lower level. Branna may have dropped into the gun deck, or the hold, but she was disoriented by the darkness.

She moved back down the corridor, her weak lantern barely lighting the floor in front of her. She found the ladder down and slowed her pace enough to ensure she didn't fall through the hatch and injure herself.

She hit the bottom and turned, holding the lantern high. The corridor on this level branched and she didn't know which way to go. She tried to get a sense of where she was, but the dark and her fear were causing her to panic. "Oh, God, where?"

"Julia."

She moved into the passageway on the left at the whispered sound of her name. It was so faint she may have imagined it. She quieted her breathing.

"Julia, help."

This whisper came again, and she hurried down the passage. She moved past storage rooms and small holds along the way, peering inside each. "Branna? Tell me where you are."

She was getting frantic. She had to be near the bow of the ship by now and probably coming up on the forward hold. She staggered as her foot dropped down an unseen step. She threw an arm out and steadied herself against the bulkhead—or what she thought was the bulkhead. It wobbled and she realized she was standing between stacks of crates.

She lowered the lantern toward the floor and illuminated the few steps down into the hold but couldn't see beyond that. She took another step down and her foot submerged in water. She extended the lantern out as far as she could. The hold was flooded, and the dim light reflected off thick bluish scum on the surface. There was no way to tell how deep it was. The bloated body of a dead rat drifted into the light and Julia straightened with a gasp.

They hadn't come this far and there was no way Branna was down here. The hair on her arms stood on end and fear gripped her heart. Branna had to be the other way.

"Julia!"

She sobbed a relieved breath and moved away from the stairs. "Branna, where are you? I can't see anything."

"Stay where you are! I'll find you."

"Help me," a voice whispered from deep in the hold.

"Is someone there?" she called, a moment before something heavy and hard slammed into her back.

Julia screamed and flailed out, trying to find a purchase and stop her fall. There was nothing and she splashed into the hold, the foul water filling her mouth and gagging her. She choked and spat putrid water from her mouth. Her clothes weighed her down, but she got her feet under her and stood in knee-high murky water and wiped slime from stinging eyes. The lantern had gone out and she wasn't sure which way led back to the steps.

"Julia!" Branna called from the corridor. "Are you all right?"

"I'm here." Julia coughed and stumbled in the dark over unseen debris, splashing back down to her hands and knees. The lantern light was glowing down the corridor and she crawled toward it, desperate to get out of the water.

"Jesus Christ!" Branna pushed fallen crates out of the way and reached for her hand to help her out. "What happened?"

"I don't know." Julia sobbed a breath.

"Are you hurt?" Branna held the lantern up and wiped grime from around her mouth and eyes.

"No. Just cold. I thought I heard someone. I thought it was you, but it wasn't, and something hit me from behind."

Branna gripped Julia's hand tightly. "We're getting the hell out of here."

She let Branna pull her along through the corridors and back to the main deck. Her clothes were soaked through and heavy and Julia was trembling hard by the time they emerged onto the main deck, which wasn't as much of an improvement as she had hoped. It was foggy *and* dark, and they were losing what little warmth was left in the air. Branna guided them to the gunwale and the rope ladder. Even if they couldn't sail in this weather, she would feel a hell of a lot better when they were back on the *Aurora*, and she could rinse off and change into dry clothes.

"I think someone else is here, Bran. I heard a voice. I heard movement. I think someone pushed me into the water." Julia's teeth were starting to chatter.

"You probably just heard me or wanted to hear me. I think you may have become disoriented and lost your balance in the dark or were struck by the crates."

"No. I got hit with something. Someone was…" She trailed off when Branna stared over the side, a look of shocked horror on her face. "What's wrong?"

Branna pulled up the line with which she had secured the sloop and held up the frayed end.

Julia lunged for the side, knowing what she was going to find—or wasn't going to find. The sloop was gone. She stared down into the hazy dark water. "Where's my boat?"

Branna dropped the line and ran the length of the starboard side. She dodged crates and lines and crossed to the port side where Julia could no longer see her but could hear her moving along the deck.

Julia's chest was tight and her skin crawled. She scratched at her arms and was chilled to the bone—and terrified. Her legs refused to support her weight any longer and she sagged to the deck, her arms wrapped tight around her middle for comfort and warmth. "Oh, my God. They cut the line."

Branna returned and crouched in front of her, running her hands up and down Julia's arms for warmth. "Who?"

"Whoever is on the ship, Bran. Whoever was down below."

"There's no one here." Branna held up the frayed end of the line. "It's old and worn and after I climbed up it just gave out. That's all."

Julia trembled from more than just cold. Branna didn't believe her. They were trapped here with no supplies and no way to navigate. She was certain there was someone else on board. Possibly the same someone responsible for the death of the entire crew.

CHAPTER TWENTY-FOUR

"She can't be far." Branna squinted out into the night. Visibility was still meager. "She has to be drifting right there, but I can't see her, damn it!"

If she could see, she was sure she could swim to the sloop and retrieve her. If she went in the water now, she could risk swimming around for hours and lose sight of both ships. It just wasn't possible. By the time the fog lifted they could be leagues apart.

The sound of the one sail flapping against the mast snapped her out of her trance. She could at least stop the *Windswept* and try and minimize the distance between them. She jumped up on the gunwale and swung herself around onto the shroud of the main mast. She didn't need to see well to navigate around a ship at sea. She swung out onto the yardarm and made ready to slash the sail down.

"Bran, wait. This may be our only intact sail. We may need it," Julia called up to her.

Branna could just make her out through the fog as she moved over to the mast and began to tug experimentally on the dangling lines.

Julia was right. She couldn't cut what may be their only chance of getting out of this mess. She waited while Julia worked her way through the mess of tangled lines and found the correct one that would lower the sail.

Branna guided the sail down, gathering it over the yardarm and tying it securely with the reef lines to protect it from any further damage. The fog grew thicker, and she couldn't see Julia at all, but in the heavy quiet air she could hear her labored breathing alternating with fits of wet, painful-sounding coughing. "Julia, hang on, I'm almost down."

Julia was leaning heavily against the gunwale at the base of the shroud. She inhaled sharply and coughed, a wet rattling sound coming from her chest. "Did you save the sail?"

Branna felt her skin, her face was flushed and clammy. "It'll do if we need it. You're feverish."

Julia shook her head. "I'm fine. We don't have time for this."

"We need to find you dry clothes." Branna eyed her up and down, her clothes clinging damply to her.

"I'm—"

"Not fine. Don't argue with me." Branna led them to an area free of refuse. She thought of suggesting they go to the captain's cabin so Julia could lie down, but she knew what Julia would say to that and she didn't blame her. Branna didn't want to be in there either. She would just have to find a way to make them comfortable on deck.

"I'm going to look around for some things we can use." Branna dropped the satchel next to Julia and pulled out a water skin. "Take some water. I'll be back in a few minutes."

Julia nodded. There was no point in arguing. They didn't know how long they would be stuck here and they would need to find what they could to help themselves. She uncapped the waterskin and took a long drink. It soothed the burning in her chest.

She pulled her legs up to her chest and hugged her knees to stay warm. Branna had taken the lantern, but she could see the light moving around in the captain's quarters and she didn't feel so alone—or so scared.

She jolted up and blinked, blearily, at Branna when she dropped a pile of blankets next to her. She must have dozed off.

Branna crouched next to her. "I found some clothes for you, too. How do you feel?"

"I'm okay. Just tired." She croaked and coughed wetly, belying her words. Her chest burned and her skin felt tight and hot.

Branna remained quiet as she helped her change into dry clothes—musty and too large but free of mold and sinister stains. The water in the hold was fouled and there was no telling what manner of creatures could have contaminated the water, making her sick. It was bad and they both knew it. There didn't seem to be any reason to discuss it.

Branna shook out one of the blankets and smoothed it out across the deck. "Sit on this. It will be warmer." She unfolded another and draped it around Julia's shoulders. "Better?"

Julia nodded. "Thank you."

"I'm sorry. This isn't really what I had in mind this morning when we left."

Julia's laugh turned into a cough. She stroked her fingers down the side of Branna's worried face. "It's not your fault. We're going to be okay."

"I know, but not if I don't find a few more things. I found another lantern, but we're running low on oil, and I need to find more. How are you doing on water?"

Julia handed her the waterskin. It was still nearly full. "You need to drink some."

"Julia, you need to drink this. You're sick."

"It's all we have."

"I'm going to find more."

Julia touched Branna's face along her hairline where she had apparently hit her head when she fell. Everything had happened so fast she hadn't had a chance to really look at her. "How bad is it?"

Branna lit the second lantern from the first. "It's fine. I have a hard head. I'm going to search below—"

"No, Branna, you can't."

"I'll be all right. I know my way around now."

Julia shook her head sharply and smothered a groan when her stomach cramped and turned with nausea. "It's too dangerous."

"It's more dangerous to do nothing."

Julia shivered, huddled beneath the blanket as Branna disappeared across the deck, swallowed up by the fog and the night.

Despite her tension and worry for Branna, the fog seemed to have seeped into her head and was muddling her thoughts. She had to get up and move around or she was going to fall asleep.

If Branna was going to search below, she could help by searching the deck. She didn't expect to find anything, as everything had been exposed to the elements for God knows how long, but it was all she could do. She threw off the blanket and started on the starboard side.

Fortunately, it took little effort for Julia to search through the crates on the deck. The wood was so rotted they came apart easily. She found rat-eaten fabrics, tools whose function she couldn't fathom, iron hardware and broken glass whose original form would forever remain a mystery. As expected, nothing useful.

"Julia."

She stiffened, hearing her name whispered on the wind. She searched the deck for the source but saw nothing and heard only the breeze ruffling through the tattered sails and water lapping against the hull. There was no one there. Branna was right; she had to be right. Julia was just losing her mind.

She dropped back onto the blanket, pulling the other around her shoulders again to get warm. Sweat beaded across her brow and she hunched over as her body was wracked with painful coughs.

She had lost all sense of time, but she didn't think it had taken more than half an hour to search the deck. Branna hadn't been below long. She was desperately thirsty but took only small sips from the waterskin. If Branna didn't find water this was all they had.

She replaced the waterskin and her fingers brushed the logbook. She set it in her lap, pulling the lantern close. Perhaps she could take her mind off their present situation and discover the truth of what happened to the *Windswept*.

The first few pages outlined the physical specifications of the *Windswept* and the names and positions of the crew. The captain's name was Gabriel Harrington, and the ship was commissioned six years ago. It was his words she was reading, penned in a small careful hand.

Somehow, learning personal information about the ship and crew made their loss more profound and the mystery behind it more disturbing. Julia shifted against the deck, feeling unsettled and tense.

She flipped through the early pages, some of them sticking together with substances she could only imagine. She skimmed entries detailing their voyages, a few skirmishes, discipline problems with the crew, and hiring and firing of new crew. All very mundane.

The lantern began to flicker, and she squinted in the weakening light. She was running out of time. More and more of the pages were glued together in clumps and those left loose were wrinkled and smeared in places. She could only make out snippets of entries now.

Trade with Tortuga Company successful. So much so that we are unexpectedly heavy and have added two extra days to our return.

The unexpected squall overnight found us ill-prepared. The mainsail has taken damage and we will be putting up for a day to effect repairs.

A search crew has been granted leave to explore this lush and bountiful island.

The repairs are complete. We await the crews' return.

The next several pages were stuck together, and Julia picked at the fragile parchment to find the next legible entry.

Symptoms began within hours. Fever and cramping.

Then madness, delusions and aggression. There are multiple injuries reported.

Julia's head swam as she tried to make sense of what she was reading. "Oh, God…"

CHAPTER TWENTY-FIVE

Branna moved quicker this time. She knew what to expect and Julia was safe, or as safe as she could be on deck. She checked every cabin, finding only clothes, personal items, and a few coins. She didn't expect more.

Anything they may find useful would be in the galley and adjacent storerooms and they hadn't made it that far before. She held the lantern out in front of her and slowed as she came to the weakened floor. The hole wasn't as large as it felt when she was falling through it, and she was able to skirt around it without trouble.

The galley was as she expected—dark, moldy, and foul— with the largest concentration of rats and roaches chewing away at rotting crates and each other. Oil for lamps, and drinkable water were her priorities. She could make it a few days, but Julia was sick and needed fluids more than anything.

She found oil immediately and sighed with relief when she hefted a half-full container. She shook the bugs from an intact, empty grain sack to carry whatever she was able to scrounge.

There was a tin of tea that was still good. If—when—she found water she could make Julia some. There were kegs of ale still partially full, with at least one dead rat floating in each. She searched every shelf, cupboard and closet but came up with nothing.

In the storage pantry empty sacks of grain and flour, long since chewed through, lay strewn about the floor. Casks lined the back bulkhead, and her hope was renewed. Two of them had the spigots snapped off—clearly empty. Thick brown sludge oozed out and glopped onto the floor at her feet from the next one.

On the floor beneath the last intact cask—and her last hope—was a small puddle that had her heart pounding. She touched her fingers to it, rubbing them together. It was water.

She stared at the spigot where a drop slowly formed before falling with a small splash to the puddle, another drop forming behind it. If this cask had been steadily dripping for a year it would surely have been empty long ago, or at least, there would be more water on the floor.

She gripped the ten-gallon cask and tried to lift it. It was nearly full. She didn't understand how this was possible unless whatever happened to the *Windswept* happened much more recently than last year. If that were true where the hell had they been? She shook off her confusion and opened the spigot, cupping her hand beneath the flow and sipping cautiously. The water was clean, fresh even, and Branna dropped to her knees, gulping in mouthfuls. She wet her hands and scrubbed her face and neck, cleaning off the worst of the grime and dried blood.

Her spirits lifted and she shut off the water and moved back to the galley to find something to fill with water and gather the other useful items. She could always make another trip, but she really didn't want to have to leave Julia again if she didn't have to.

Branna picked her way carefully back to the deck, unable to hold the light steady and keep the sack of precious supplies safe at the same time. The fog was still thick, but she could make out Julia hunched over against the gunwale. "Julia, I'm here."

Julia didn't reply but lurched to her feet and backed away.

"I found oil and…What's wrong?" She set the sack carefully on the deck.

"Stay back," Julia snapped.

"Why? What's happened?"

"They were sick. Don't come any closer."

"Who was sick? Julia, talk to me. Tell me what's going on."

"The crew was sick. It's in the log. It must be what killed them." Julia swayed, steadying herself against the gunwale. Her whole body trembled.

"You know I won't do that," Branna said and moved closer.

Julia's every breath seemed an effort. "Please, Branna, don't."

"If I was going to get sick it would have happened already. Let me help you."

If she was going to protest again, she never got the chance as her legs gave out and she sagged to the deck. Branna got her arms around her, easing Julia back onto the blankets, rolling one beneath her head and covering her with another.

The heat of fever radiated off her and Branna brushed damp hair from her face. Her heartbeat was strong and steady, but her breathing was labored and wheezing, an obvious infection in her chest.

Branna lifted Julia's head and touched the mouth of the waterskin to her lips. "You need to drink, machree."

Julia was weak and disoriented but able to take water with help. Satisfied she had done all she could for the moment, Branna settled her against the blankets.

"Bran, you need to go."

Branna held Julia's hand. "Julia, hush. I'm not going anywhere. Even if I wanted to."

Branna gritted her teeth against a scream of rage at their situation. If they were in port or on the *Banshee*, she could take care of her and Julia could fight this thing off. She'd even settle for the *Aurora*. Out here with barely enough to survive, Julia was in real danger and Branna felt beyond helpless.

She could only do what she could do. She retrieved the sack and emptied the contents. She had collected an iron pot, which she filled with wood from the broken crates and started a fire. It would help keep Julia warm, and when there were enough coals, allow her to heat water for tea in a smaller pot she took as well. When the fog lifted it would also be their signal fire.

She added oil to the lanterns and turned up the light. It helped dispel some of the chill and helped her feel slightly more in control. As the light radiated out, she saw the logbook. She wanted to know what Julia was so upset about.

It wasn't hard to find the passages Julia had read as so much of the book was damaged. She read through them a few times and could see why Julia was frightened, especially feeling as poorly as she was, but Branna was not convinced.

She needed to know more. She hadn't brought her throwing knives, but she had helped herself to a long, thin filleting knife from the galley and she used it now to work at separating the pages.

She managed to work a few of the pages free, but not without damage and many of Captain Harrington's final words would be lost forever. She flipped to the pages prior to the discussion of illness.

The crew are all experienced, fit, and well-armed. They have not been ashore long, yet my unease grows with every passing moment. The island which at first appeared a utopia…

….the men who survived are all aboard. Two were lost in the bush, three more on the beach—Their screams still echo in my ears.

The crew is shaken…

…the attack from the inhabitants was swift and brutal…. discolored wounds suspicious for poison…

Poison. She was now up to the page Julia had read. They *were* sick but not the way Julia thought. The men had been poisoned by inhabitants of the island they were exploring.

"Bran," Julia rasped.

"Aye." She touched Julia's face and nearly jerked her hand back. She was burning up. "Julia, I'm here. You're going to be all right."

Branna was feeling less and less convinced of that. She tore up a section of blanket and soaked it in water which wasn't at all cool, but compared to Julia's skin, probably felt like ice as she draped it across her head and wiped sweat from her neck and chest.

Julia's eyes opened, unfocused and bright. "Hope you're taking good care of my boat. I want to give Kit a good report when we return."

"Aye, machree." Branna's chest tightened with fear. "Please, try and drink more."

Julia nodded, her eyes drifting closed while Branna held the water for her, and she managed several long swallows before coughing and choking up the last little bit. She looked at Branna again, blinking in surprise. "You found water?"

"Yes. And oil and I started a fire." She nodded her head in the direction of the pot of crackling wood.

Julia followed Branna's gaze and smiled slightly, lifting her hand for a moment toward the warmth before it dropped down on the blanket. "You think of everything."

Branna smiled around the fear in her heart, hiding her worry by rewetting the cloth and wiping Julia's face. She worked to control her own breathing and ease the tightness in her chest. "I read some more of the log. The men weren't sick with disease. They were attacked. Poisoned, I think."

"Attacked?"

"Aye. I'm not sure of the details but they stopped for repairs outside Tortuga. I don't know the island. I need to look at the charts and go through the log. They must have recorded it somewhere. Only part of the crew was affected. I still don't know what happened to them, or where the ship has been, or how the hell it got here for that matter, but I'm hoping I can decipher more of the log and then..." Julia was asleep again.

Branna pulled the blanket up to Julia's chest and tucked her arms beneath. She broke up more wood for the fire, trying to ensure Julia would be as warm and comfortable as possible. She needed to spend some time in the captain's quarters again and see if she could make sense of his charts.

Julia didn't appear to be in any immediate danger, but Branna was torn. Stay with her, make sure she was safe and ease her mind, or leave her again for a short time and do what she could to get them off this bloody ship and get Julia the care she needed—and maybe discover what had happened to the ship and crew. It was decided.

Branna set the lantern on the floor and righted the navigation table. One of the legs was broken and it wobbled precariously but it would hold if she didn't lean on it too much. She eyed the mess on the floor. Some of the charts were undamaged and she collected those first. She unrolled each one carefully, studying it for a moment to confirm what she suspected would be true. The charts she needed were going to be the damaged ones.

She set to work gathering the torn and scattered charts from the floor. It was slow with the poor light and delicate paper, but she made every effort not to damage them further. She stacked the pieces carefully on the navigation table and began the laborious process of piecing them back together. She intended to have more answers when Julia woke again.

CHAPTER TWENTY-SIX

Julia was so hot. She struggled her arms out from under the blanket, pulling it down from her chest. Her mouth was desperately dry. If she could just get some water she would feel better, but she couldn't drag her eyes open and it felt like someone was sitting on her chest. It was so hard to catch her breath. The deck creaked nearby.

"Bran?" she whispered hoarsely and cracked her eyes. Her vision was hazy, but she could see movement and sense someone near.

The cool cloth felt so good across her brow. Julia sighed and turned her head into the gentle caress down her face. "Branna, I'm so hot."

"I know," a deep voice rumbled.

A figure loomed over her with dark, twisted features. Her heart hammered in her chest and fear gripped her as she struggled to focus. She knew this face, but it was impossible. She tried to turn away from the touch.

"Do not fear, Julia. I will take care of you."

"You're dead," she breathed when she looked into the ruined face of Captain Isaac Shaw.

He smiled but only one side of his face moved. The left side was paralyzed and misshapen. He was missing an eye, the socket crusted over and seeping with ragged, poorly healed tears in the skin. His mouth was torn, teeth broken, and sections of scalp torn off and partially healed over with gnarled scar tissue. "As you will soon be, too."

Terror surged through her, and Julia struggled to push herself up. This wasn't real. This couldn't be real. She groped for her cutlass, the quick movement as she lurched to her feet turning her stomach. She spun and swayed, nearly falling to the deck as she waved her blade erratically in his direction. "Stay away from me! You're dead! I killed you!"

Captain Shaw stood hunched, his left arm hanging at an unnatural angle, his left leg bowed in, splinted with planks of wood and tied with rags. "Death cannot keep me from you. We were meant for each other."

"I'm not dead. I'm going to live. And you can go to hell!" She screamed and charged as he disappeared into the fog.

Branna finally found the missing section of the charts she wanted. The first, the area around Nassau which she knew like the back of her hand, but who knew how far they would've drifted by the time they could navigate again? The second, the waters around Tortuga. She needed to know where the *Windswept* had been. She wanted to find that island and find the truth about what happened to her crew.

She collected the pages and tucked them under her arm when she heard Julia scream. Her head whipped toward the deck, and she took off out the door. She skidded to a stop at the empty blankets. She tucked the charts safely into the logbook and whirled when she heard Julia scream again, the sound bouncing around through the fog.

"Show yourself, you son of a bitch!" Julia slashed wildly.

"Whoa! Whoa! Easy!" Branna jumped back, narrowly missing being run through as Julia lunged for her. She held her hands out from her sides to show she was unarmed. She couldn't fathom what set Julia off but thought, perhaps, she was hallucinating. "It's me, it's Branna."

"Branna, arm yourself!"

"Julia, I'm not going to fight you."

"Not me!" Julia stayed on guard, peering into the night, tensing and jumping at every sound. "Captain Shaw."

"What? Julia, Shaw is—"

"He's here. He's come for me."

She was delirious with fever. "Julia, please, put down your blade."

"No! Branna, draw your sword," she pleaded before being overcome with a fit of coughing.

Branna stepped closer. "Julia, you're sick. You're not thinking clearly. Please, put down your weapon."

"You must believe me. He'll kill us both."

"Julia, I promise you. I won't let anything happen to you." Branna's heart broke for her. She was so unwell and so scared.

"I won't let him win. I won't be a victim." Julia turned and screamed into the night, "Do you hear me, you bastard!"

Branna closed the distance between them and wrapped her arms around her from behind, pinning Julia's arms at her sides.

"What are you doing?"

"I'm sorry, machree." Branna applied pressure to Julia's wrists. "Forgive me."

"Branna, you're hurting me." Julia's grip loosened and the cutlass clattered to the deck. "Let me go."

"I'm so sorry. I won't let anything happen to you. I love you."

"Branna, don't do this. You must believe me," she begged and struggled against Branna's hold.

Branna held her tightly until her legs gave out and her ragged breathing evened as she slipped unconscious. As carefully as she could, she slung Julia over her shoulder and carried her back to their makeshift camp, lowering her to the blankets.

Branna raked her hands through her hair and sat back on her heels, sweat from tension and exertion trickling down her brow. Julia was pale and her breathing shallow and wheezing.

The pulse jumping at her neck was fast and irregular. Her body was working too hard to fight this infection and Branna didn't know how long she could keep it up—if her fever didn't break soon. She couldn't think about that now.

She arranged Julia under the blankets again and stoked the fire which had burned down to embers, tossing more wood on. It blazed back to life, throwing off heat and light. Branna grabbed the waterskin and sucked down a few mouthfuls before getting more into Julia. She could at least keep fluids in her.

Branna settled next to her with the logbook and the charts. By morning she expected the fog would have burned off and she intended to have the answers she needed by then and some way to get them home.

The *Windswept* was on route from Tortuga to Nassau when they were blown of course far enough that it now made Port Royal their closer port. Branna shuffled through the sections of chart, turning them over in her hand and holding them to the light to find the correct sections and orient herself.

She could see a faint line drawn across the chart where Harrington had estimated their new location. She shuffled the pages again to find the corresponding section so she could follow the line. It was tedious and her eyes burned from strain with poor light and exhaustion.

The line stopped in the next section, faded out and disappeared in a poorly charted channel of shallow water and shoals southwest of Tortuga. It was treacherous water for the big ships with too much draw. The *Windswept* would never have sailed through there deliberately. Branna was satisfied she had a general idea where they had been forced to stop for repairs. She tucked the relevant charts back in the log and the rest into the satchel.

She opened the logbook again. Where was the crew and how did the ship get here? Wherever *here* was. If all she had was the log, she could easily assume the *Windswept* never made it off the island or out of the channel. Except, she was sitting on the deck of the ship, so what happened between then and now?

She turned to where she had stopped reading before and skimmed the sections again about the crew getting sick, becoming bedridden and then turning violent. She had heard of poisons that affected people both physically and mentally, causing hallucinations. She peeled more pages apart with the knife before jamming it into the deck nearby.

...the first attacks came as the crew off watch were sleeping... slaughtered in their bunks by their shipmates...

...I can hear the fighting even now...

Mr. Blythe and a few men struggle to keep the ship on course to Port Royal and help.

The next few pages were hopelessly stuck together and there were thick dark splotches staining the pages. Blood. The next legible page was clearly written in another's hand.

We couldn't maintain course and protect the captain. He was murdered by three crewmen.

We won't make Port Royal. Only a few of us not affected are still alive. We won't expose innocent people to this horror...

...making for the islands north of Port Royal. The rocky north beach will protect the ship...

"Bloody hell." It was the last entry and Branna snapped the book closed. They had been right on top of her only a few weeks ago. Countless ships would have stopped at the island. The protected south cove was a well-used haven and now the final resting place of the *Ferryman*. The north side was rocky and treacherous with unpredictable currents, unexplored threads, inlets, and caves. The *Windswept* would never have been found. So how was it found?

Julia moaned. "Branna?"

"Aye." Branna reached for her hand under the blanket. "Are you with me?"

Julia sighed and licked her lips. "Water?"

Branna held the waterskin while she drank until water spilled down her face and neck and she began to cough. "Easy."

"Thank you."

"How do you feel?" She felt Julia's face. Still dangerously hot but her eyes seemed clear for the moment.

"Branna, you need to listen to me. Please, I'm begging you, you must believe me. I know I'm sick, but I know what I saw. I wasn't hallucinating. Captain Shaw is here."

"Julia—"

"He's here. He's been here. You heard the same noises I did below. I heard someone calling my name before. I thought it was you and it was him. How is this ship sailing? Explain that."

Branna searched her eyes. They were bright with fever and determination. Julia was so certain, and she seemed, at least now, to be clearheaded. Branna did hear something before but brushed it off as falling crates. The lost sloop. The rope was sound when she climbed up. Did it break after, or could it have been cut? She never heard Julia's name, but did that mean it wasn't true? She couldn't explain the fresh water and now she knew the ship had been hidden for a year on the island where she last saw Captain Isaac Shaw. Could he have survived that fall and discovered the ship? It still seemed completely absurd.

"Branna, you must be ready. I can't lose you. Please, tell me you'll be ready."

"Aye." Branna gripped her hand and brushed hair out of her face. She still didn't know what to think but Julia was so certain. "I'll be ready. I'll look around."

"He's hurt. His whole left side…only one eye, his face his scarred. His arm and leg maimed…" Julia's eyes drifted closed.

Her description was so detailed, and he certainly wouldn't have survived that fall uninjured. Fear tightened her chest. "Julia." Branna gave her shoulder a small shake. "Was he armed?" The part of her that refused to believe he was alive and terrorizing them on the long missing *Windswept* cringed at the question. The rest of her needed to know.

Julia's eyes fluttered open again and she coughed. "I don't know."

Branna winced at the painful sound of her breathing. "It's okay. Just rest. I'll take care of it."

"Be careful," Julia whispered.

Branna watched her for a moment before sitting back and cocking her head to listen. It was time to take this seriously. If

Julia was wrong and Branna was chasing a ghost, there was no one here to see. If she was right, then Branna had unfinished business with Captain Shaw.

She listened to the fog-muted night sounds. Creaking wood, lapping water and loose lines blowing against the mast. Now there was the crackling of the fire and Julia's breathing. She heard nothing unexpected, but now she felt a real sense of unease.

Branna rose and turned to face the deck, opening herself up and turning all her senses outward. She didn't close her eyes but let them go unfocused. Visibility was as bad as ever and the fog hung heavy in the air, cooling and creeping along her skin and muffling sound.

She drew her sword, the blade singing as it came free of the scabbard. If he was out there, he heard and he knew she was coming for him. She wanted to search the deck, but she couldn't lose sight of Julia. If Julia had her cutlass to hand, Branna would feel better about searching the deck.

"Damn." She hadn't recovered it from the deck when she'd forced it from Julia's hands. It didn't matter. Julia wouldn't be able to use it anyway.

She began a slow sweep of the deck back and forth out from where Julia lay, never letting her out of her sight and working farther out with each pass. She stopped at every end of her arc and listened. If he was as injured as Julia said he would have to take her by surprise. Branna had no intention of letting that happen. She would force him out.

"I know you're out there, Shaw. I can smell your cowardice." She drew the last word out with a sneer and let it hang in the air.

The fire hissed and popped behind her as her eyes swept across the deck, straining to pick up a hint of movement.

"And I your arrogance," he said from within the fog.

She was careful not to react though her heart leapt into her throat and her grip went white-knuckled around the hilt. She hadn't yet truly believed. She turned in the direction from which she thought he had spoken. "Show yourself."

"How long before Julia grows weary of your strong-arm tactics and patronization?" His voice was slurred, like speaking was an effort.

Branna bristled at his words. She had been wrong and had failed to trust Julia again and had hurt her under the guise of keeping her safe.

"Truth hurts doesn't it, Captain?"

Branna's head whipped to the left. He had moved and she wondered if he was as injured as Julia suggested. "I can live with my truth, Shaw. Can you?" She moved out farther onto the deck. As long as she kept him in front of her and Julia behind her, she could manage. The farther she moved, though, the more room it gave him to come around behind her. She had to keep him talking.

His laugh was harsh and gurgling. "Why don't you enlighten me, Captain?"

He was still in front of her and she moved out another step. "You're a monster, Shaw, and now everyone who looks at you will know it. You can't hide behind slick words and a charming smile, can you?"

Her comment was met with silence. Branna stayed still and listened, hearing nothing but the wind and water. She looked back at the starboard gunwale. She could see the fire, but it was hazy through the fog, and she couldn't make out Julia at all. She had come too far.

Shaw was trying to separate them, draw Branna away from her but he would still need to fight her first if he was going to get to Julia and she knew she could take him. What was he really after? If he had wanted to hurt Julia, he could have done so already. Branna had left her unprotected more than once.

"Gotcha!" His voice came from somewhere close and behind her.

She spun and lunged in the direction, taking two steps before her right foot broke through a weak area in the deck and she lurched forward onto her hands as her leg plunged through the broken planks.

Branna couldn't help a gasp of pain as the sharp wood ripped through her pants and cut into her flesh along the inside of her thigh. She slapped her hands down onto the deck, releasing her grip on her sword to stop herself from going all the way through again, and tried to lever herself out.

The wood end, embedded in her skin, dug deeper as she pulled at her leg. "No. Damn it!"

"You're so predictable, Captain. That was far too easy. I know this ship like my own. It is my own."

Branna ceased struggling and listened, trying to get a location on him. He had moved away from her and toward where she left Julia, her worst nightmare coming to life. "Stay away from her!"

"It was a pleasure to see you again, Captain."

Branna gripped her sword, using the hilt to bash at the broken planks trapping her leg. "Julia! Julia, get up!"

Seconds ticked by that seemed endless as she pounded away at the broken planks. She loosened the wood, breaking it off and twisting her leg free just when she heard a rustle of movement and a struggle. Wood grated against wood, the fire popped and sparked and there was a grunt of surprise followed by an inhuman shriek that chilled her to the bone. There was a tremendous splash, then deafening silence.

Branna froze, her breath sucked from her lungs, and terror she'd never known gripped her soul as she made her way across the deck.

A form was standing at the gunwale and Branna exhaled a shuddering breath when she saw Julia gazing out over the sea. "Julia?"

"The fog is beginning to lift."

Branna frowned. Had Shaw gone over? "What happened?"

"Where's my boat?" Julia asked before she collapsed to the deck.

CHAPTER TWENTY-SEVEN

"Julia!" Branna dropped to her knees and pulled Julia into her arms. Her hair was sticky with blood which had sprayed and splattered across her face and dripped down her chest. Her right hand still gripped the filleting knife and blood coated her hands and arms, dripping onto the deck.

Branna pulled at her shirt, running her hands over her neck and chest, checking for injuries. She felt along her abdomen, sides, and slipped her hands down her back. "You're okay. You're okay."

She pried the knife out of her hand and tossed it away, pushing up her sleeves and examining her hands and arms. She found nothing but she could tell more if she got her cleaned up. "Julia? Can you hear me?"

She was burning up. Branna moved her back over to the blankets, not far from where she'd fallen and settled her back down. Before she could attend any more to Julia, she needed to make sure the ship was secure. She had insisted they were alone before, and it almost cost them both their lives.

She took a step and pain shot up her leg. She gripped her thigh and blood immediately seeped through her fingers. "Bloody hell." She shrugged out of her scabbard and slid off the leather shoulder strap, winding it tightly around her leg above the wound. It would do for now.

Branna peered over the side. She didn't expect to see a body, but she had to check. She could see farther now. Julia was right, the fog was lifting.

Her jaw clenched in tension and her sword gripped tightly, she made a thorough sweep of the deck. Every passing moment the fog thinned, allowing her to see more of the ship at one time.

She recovered Julia's cutlass as she checked behind every crate and opened every hatch, peering down and listening before slamming it shut and barricading it with crates. It wouldn't keep someone down for long, but it would make a lot of noise if it were opened.

She checked the captain's quarters. No hidden rooms. No Captain Shaw. He was gone for good this time, and when Julia recovered, maybe she could tell her about it. Branna didn't know what had happened, but from what she heard and the amount of blood, she could imagine. She dug up another shirt and returned to the deck.

Julia didn't stir as Branna stripped off her bloody shirt and cleaned the worst of the blood from her skin and hair. She was too sick to know what was happening.

She broke up more wood for the fire, drank water and got some into Julia. She had no idea what time it was, but the night air was so dark and still she suspected it was only hours before dawn. The fog continued to lift as she lay down next to Julia, pulling her close with a protective arm around her.

Branna dragged her eyes open, grainy and sore from exhaustion. She blinked up at the bright blue sky and felt sunlight warming her skin. The breeze was high and the ship rocked gently in the swells.

She ached and when she shifted her leg, there was a biting pain. She sat up with a start. Julia was so still but only warm to the touch, her hair plastered to her skin and her shirt soaked through. Her fever was breaking. The tightness of fear in Branna's chest eased and she listened to the slow, strong pulse. Julia's breathing was deep and rattled less.

"Come along her starboard side!"

Branna struggled to her feet when the shouted command carried to her on the breeze. She shielded her eyes from the day's brightness to see the most beautiful sight she'd ever seen. The *Banshee* was pulling in her sails and coming alongside.

"Ahoy the ship!" Gus called as he stood on the gunwale and stared, surprised and confused. "Branna?"

The crew threw the boarding hooks and secured the ships together while they all gaped at their captain and shouted amongst themselves about this ship being the *Windswept.*

"Quiet!" Gus bellowed at the excited crew. "Captain, are you all right? Where's Julia?"

Branna sagged against the gunwale, exhaustion and relief overwhelming her. "She's here. She's sick."

"Get them aboard!" Gus ordered. "Secure that ship!"

The crew exploded into action and swarmed the *Windswept.* Branna lost sight of Julia as she disappeared beneath the attention of Jack, Nat, and enough crewmen to carry her safely over to the *Banshee.*

Gus swung across the gunwale to Branna, taking in the belt around her leg and bloodstained pants. "Can you walk?"

"Aye." Branna went to gather up their weapons and the satchel.

"Let me." Gus took their gear and held a hand for her to help her up to the gunwale.

She accepted gratefully. They were going home.

"Christ! Take it easy, man." Branna jumped and gripped the arms of the chair, gritting her teeth when Gus sent the needle through the sensitive skin of her inner thigh to close up the ragged wound.

"Hold still. You said you didn't want to wait for Jack, so this is what you get," he muttered.

She sighed and took a pull from the bottle of rum, her gaze flicking to the bed where Jack sat tending to Julia with Nat hovering nearby. They had managed to rouse her briefly and get her to drink. They cleaned her up and helped her change into her own clean clothes before she slipped away again into sleep without ever really seeming to know where she was or what was happening.

Her fever was hanging on while her body continued to fight whatever infection was in that water, but it was no longer dangerously high. She would be all right with time and rest.

"Talk to me then." Branna winced as he jabbed her again. "How did you find us?"

"We were heading back in when the fog settled. We dropped sail and held course as best we could overnight. When it lifted, we near ran over this little sloop adrift."

Branna jumped and Gus stabbed her in the leg. "Aw, fuck. You have Julia's boat?"

"Yes. Though we didn't know it was Julia's at the time. Do we need to talk about this after?"

Branna settled back down and tried to relax. "No, go on."

Gus eyed her for another moment before getting back to work. "After we searched her, we started wondering. We saw the damage to the hull and knew you'd struck something. We assumed…"

They thought they had gone over and been lost. She would have thought the same. "I understand."

Gus cleared his throat. "We sent Harris aloft with the spyglass and saw the ship. You were right in the middle of the shipping lane. If not us, someone else would have spotted you before long."

"Thank Christ."

Gus was quiet for a long time as he worked on her leg, finishing up the stitches and wrapping around a clean bandage. "What happened to you, Branna?"

Branna looked from him to Nat and Jack and all eyes were on her. "The ship came upon us in the fog. We collided but we were okay. We caught up with her and boarded to investigate. I recognized her as the *Windswept* right away. We found the ship's log. It's in rough shape but it explains what happened to her."

"What happened to Julia?" Jack asked. "How did she get so sick?"

"We were searching below, and I fell through a weak spot in the floor onto the gun deck. She went down looking for me and we got separated. There was putrid water in the hold, and she fell in."

Jack grimaced. "And the blood on Julia? All over the deck? It was yours?"

Branna took a deep breath and another swallow of rum. "No."

The word hung in the air for a long time before Gus spoke. "Branna, what aren't you telling us?"

"Are you done?" Branna gestured to her leg.

Gus tied off the bandage. "Yes."

She stood and picked up the satchel pulling out the log. She flipped to the page that began the *Windswept*'s troubles and handed it to Gus before limping over to the bed. Jack moved so she could sit down next to Julia. She was alarmingly pale still but seemed to be resting comfortably.

Jack and Nat moved to stand over each shoulder and read along with Gus. "Where is this island?" Nat asked.

Branna pointed to the satchel. "I recovered their charts and pieced them back together. I have a pretty good idea how to find it."

"Jesus," Jack said. "I've heard of toxins like this, hallucinogens that can be made from plant extracts, or some animals—insects or frogs, maybe?"

"Bloody hell!" Gus blurted. "We were right on top of them. I mean, dozens of ships could have seen them if they had traveled around to the north side of the island."

"But no one ever does," Nat said. "It seems like that's why Alden Blythe chose that spot. To be out of the way. To protect people. He did a remarkable thing."

Gus sat back against the navigation table and crossed his arms. "If they've been beached or wedged in a grotto for a year, why are we seeing her now?"

"The storm," Nat suggested. "The storm freed her up and she drifted out."

"She wasn't adrift," Branna said. "There was someone else on board."

Gus straightened. "A survivor?"

Branna pressed her lips together in a hard line, her eyes flicking again to Julia. She hadn't stirred, her breathing deep and even. "In a manner of speaking."

"Branna, what the hell?" Gus snapped.

"Isaac Shaw didn't die on that island. The fall didn't kill him. I don't know how, maybe the jungle broke his fall, a deep pool or a wild boar, who the hell knows? He found the ship, rigged a sail and got out. I don't know what he had planned, but he found us."

They gaped at her, eyes huge in disbelief. Jack recovered first. "Captain, that's cra—"

"I know. Believe me, I know how it sounds. I didn't believe either and I almost got Julia killed. I almost got us both killed."

Gus's expression turned from disbelief to enraged in a flash. "You took care of it, I assume."

She laughed, bitterly. "I didn't touch him. I never even saw him."

"There was so much blood," Jack said.

Branna raised Julia's hand to her lips, brushing a soft kiss across the back of her hand. "I know. I saw the blood. I heard it happen."

"Julia killed him? How?" Gus asked.

"I don't know," Branna said. "I don't even know if Julia will. She was delirious from fever, barely conscious all night. That's why I didn't…that's why I didn't believe her. I left her alone and she tried to tell me. She tried to tell me someone was on the ship. That it was Shaw, and I didn't believe her."

"Captain, you couldn't have known," Nat said.

"I could have trusted her. And I let her down again."

"Maybe she won't even remember," Jack muttered, his eyes widening as Branna shot him a withering look. "I didn't mean about…I mean killing Shaw or whatever…"

"So, what now?" Nat asked. "What about the *Windswept*? Is she salvageable?"

"Where are we anyway?" Branna asked.

"We're only a day out," Gus said.

"Let's tow her back." Branna looked between them. "I think she should sail again."

"I'll see to it." Gus motioned for Nat and Jack to follow him out, leaving Branna alone with Julia.

"You're going to be fine, machree. We're going home."

CHAPTER TWENTY-EIGHT

Julia bolted up with a strangled gasp, a hand to her chest. Her breath came fast and terror gripped her heart while her gaze darted around the room.

Her room. Branna's room. She was at Travers in her bed and a gorgeous setting sun streaked through the window and a soft, warm breeze fluttered the drapes. She shook her head, her eyes closed tight to shake the fog from her brain. Her throat was painfully dry, her head ached savagely, and her body felt leaden and weak.

One thing at a time. She reached a shaky hand for the glass of water on the nightstand and drained it far too fast, coughing on the last few swallows. She swung her legs out of bed and pushed herself to stand. She swayed slightly, her hand pressing against the bridge of her nose to try and ease the ache behind her eyes. She felt terrible and all the worse for her confusion.

She staggered to the door, dressed only in her shift.

Despite Dr. Tuttle's assurances that Julia would be fine with rest and fluids, Branna drummed her fingers on the table while the conversation buzzed around her. The *Banshee* was once again the talk of the port as she sailed into Nassau towing the long-lost *Windswept*.

They dropped off both the *Windswept* and Julia's sloop at the repair docks. Family and friends of the *Windswept*'s crew were coming out from all corners demanding answers, demanding to be let on the ship.

Genevieve knew the families and fielded their questions as best she could. She had read the log and had the same information as anyone else. She had instructed the repair foreman to allow them on the ship as soon as it was safe to begin going through the personal effects of their loved ones, and an officer from the *Banshee*—Genevieve had nominated Nat—would be on hand to supervise. By the laws of salvage, the *Windswept* and all she held belonged to Captain Kelly now and no one would dare challenge that fact.

"So, Julia sliced an' diced Captain Shaw with a filleting knife an' threw 'is body overboard?" Merri blurted as she heard the story for the first time.

Branna frowned and stared up at their door. Julia had not awakened at all during the remaining sail home or her litter transport from the ship to their room this morning and Branna was on the verge of panic.

"I didn't see what happened," she said and continued to stare up, regretting that she had let them convince her to leave Julia's bedside and come down for something to eat.

"Oy, Julia sure does 'ave a dark side. Ya must be rubbin' off—"

"Enough!" Branna's hand slammed onto the table as she shot her a chilling look. She was sickened by what she knew must have happened and her guts twisted at the thought that Julia may not remember and equally that she may.

"Branna." Genevieve placed a hand on her arm, her gaze flicking up to the balcony.

Branna followed her gaze to see Julia standing unsteadily at the railing. She jumped up, taking the stairs two at a time, heedless of her still healing leg.

Julia was trembling, tears streaking down her face, unchecked. Branna pulled Julia into her arms, her body wracked with wrenching sobs. She clung to Branna desperately, burying her face in Branna's neck.

Branna held her tightly, running her hands up and down her back. "You shouldn't be out of bed."

"I don't know what's hap…happening."

"It's okay," Branna soothed and pulled away enough to guide Julia back to their room. "I'm sorry I wasn't here when you woke up."

Julia took a few shuddering breaths and let Branna sit her on the edge of the bed. "How long have we been here? How did we get here?"

"Maybe you should lie down," Branna said.

"I feel like I've been asleep for days."

"You have." Branna pulled a blanket from the end of the bed and wrapped it around Julia's shoulders. "How much do you remember?"

"Um…" Julia pinched the bridge of her nose in obvious pain. "I don't, um, everything is so muddled, like a dream."

"It's all right. The doctor said you may not remember everything right away. It may come back in bits and pieces."

"Doctor?"

"You've been really sick for a few days but you're going to be fine."

"I fell into the water," she murmured. "The *Windswept*. We were trapped on the ship. You fell through the deck."

"Yes, but I'm fine."

"We were out on my boat. We talked. We were together. The *Aurora*?"

"She's here. The *Banshee* picked her up after the fog lifted. That's how they knew to look for us. The sloop is being repaired."

"The fog. That's right, I remember."

Julia looked far away for a long time and Branna chewed her lip waiting, tensely, for the moment it all came rushing back to her. She looked like she was struggling to put it all together before her face finally relaxed and she blew out a slow breath.

"The *Banshee* picked us up? How far had we drifted?" she asked.

"Not far. We were still in the shipping lane and would have been found fast by someone."

"That's good for us, right?"

"Yes," Branna agreed and touched the back of her hand to Julia's face. "Your temperature has returned to normal. How do you feel?"

"Terrible, actually. Mostly tired and weak, I guess. And hungry."

"Hungry? That's good. I'll get you something." Branna rose to leave.

Julia gripped her arm, her eyes widening in alarm. "Don't leave."

"I'll be back soon." She pried Julia's hand off her arm and held it for a moment. "I'll just be downstairs."

"I'm sorry," she whispered. "I don't know what's wrong with me."

"It's okay. I'm going to get you something to eat and let everyone know you're doing okay."

"Am I? Doing okay? Because I don't feel okay, Bran."

"Give yourself some time, machree," Branna said. "We'll talk it through. I'll be back shortly."

"How is she?" Genevieve asked when Branna came back down.

"Hungry," Branna said and slumped down into her chair.

Genevieve waved a serving girl over and instructed her to bring them a plate of food and clean water for Julia.

"How much does she remember?" Jack asked.

"I'm not sure. She seems to remember being out on the sloop, the fog and the *Windswept*. She remembers falling into the water in the hold and she remembers I fell through the deck. She didn't say anything about Shaw, but it's obvious she knows there's more."

"Is she okay?" Gus asked.

"No, I don't think she is. She seems, I don't know, lost and scared but doesn't know why and I don't know how much I should tell her."

"I don't think you should tell her anything," Jack said.

"You can't keep this from her," Nat said.

"I think she's not remembering because she's not ready to yet," Jack explained. "And I don't think you should force it."

Branna shook her head. "I don't know."

"Maybe instead of tellin' 'er, ya just help 'er remember on 'er own," Merriam suggested.

It wasn't often she took advice from Merriam, but Branna was willing to consider anything to help Julia. "What do you mean?"

"Take 'er back ta the ship. When she's feelin' better, o' course. But don't let this go on too long."

They all looked at Merriam with varying levels of surprise at her thoughtfulness and insight. Jack slipped his arm around her and gave her a squeeze, kissing the top of her head.

The serving girls had prepared everything Gen had asked for and Branna carried it carefully up the stairs. She toed open the door to the room, her arms laden down with a tray of food and every possible beverage that Julia may want, along with warm fresh water for washing. Genevieve had tried to have the serving girls carry it for her, but Branna sensed Julia wasn't ready to see anyone else yet.

She regretted not leaving it to the professionals when she almost upended the entire tray crossing the room. Glasses clinked and tipped over and water sloshed out onto the floor before she could get the tray down on the table. "Bloody hell."

Despite the clatter, Julia didn't move from the balcony doors where she stood watching the last of the sun's rays disappear behind the horizon.

"Julia?" Branna said, worried at the faraway look in her eyes and the way she hugged herself, running her hands up and down her arms as if for warmth.

She still did not respond and Branna placed a hand on her arm. Her skin was ice-cold and Branna jerked her hand back when Julia jumped at the touch. "Julia, you're freezing."

"I can't shake this chill," she whispered. "It feels like it's in my bones."

Branna collected the blanket from the floor where Julia must have dropped it and draped it over her shoulders again.

"Thank you."

She gestured to the tray. "Will you try and eat something?"

"Yes." Julia slid onto a chair and thoroughly explored everything Branna brought up.

Branna had already eaten and poured herself a glass of rum. For Julia she made hot tea and splashed a shot of rum in it before sliding it across the table to her. "This should help warm you."

"Thank you," Julia said around a mouthful of food.

Branna was pleased she felt well enough to eat. It could only help. "Do you want to talk about anything?"

Julia didn't hesitate and straightened in her chair. "I think we need to help the families of the *Windswept's* crew find peace and closure with what has happened."

That was not what Branna had expected her to say, but she had the same thought. She couldn't help the *Windswept's* crew at the time, but she could help their loved ones now. "I agree. How?"

"Go back to the island near Port Royal and find the bodies, if there are any, and give them a proper burial for one. You said the ship is at the repair yard? Getting it restored and sailing again would help. Was there money aboard? We never really got a good look...at the...at the..."

"Julia?" Something was wrong. The pulse was pounding at Julia's throat and a thin sheen of sweat beaded across her brow.

"I'm sorry." She pushed back from the table and stood abruptly. "I need to lie down."

"It's okay. Don't worry. You still have some healing to do." Branna helped her to the bed.

Julia curled on her side, her head pillowed on her arm so she could see out through the balcony doors to the sunset. "Are you going to stay?"

"Of course. I'll be right here."

CHAPTER TWENTY-NINE

Branna knew what the night was going to bring but she was still startled awake at Julia's first cry. Her brow was furrowed with tension and her eyes moved erratically behind tightly closed lids. Branna wanted more than anything to wake her and spare her from reliving it in her dreams, but Julia needed to remember, or it would haunt her until she did.

Branna sat up in the bed to give Julia some space. Julia's hands twisted into the bedsheets and the muscles in her neck strained as she clenched her jaw. She couldn't stand it any longer and touched her shoulder. "Julia, wake up."

Julia lashed out violently at Branna's touch and her eyes flew open. "No!" she gasped, panting and clutching blindly for Branna. She covered her face with her hands.

"It's just a dream. You're safe now," Branna said.

Julia took a shuddering breath. "It's not just a dream. Is it?"

Branna pulled Julia to her, wrapping her arms around her and holding her tight. "You don't have to do this alone. You're not alone."

Branna held Julia as she wept bitterly for several minutes until exhausted, and she fell back to sleep once again. Branna sighed, swallowing the tightness in her throat, and settled back down next to her. She wasn't letting her go again.

Branna slept lightly, attuned to every change in Julia's breathing and every twitch of her muscles, holding her close and whispering words of love and comfort the whole night through to keep nightmares or memories at bay and let Julia get some rest.

"Talk to me, please," Branna finally said, tightening her arms around Julia's waist. She had felt her wake with the dawn a while ago but didn't want to rush her.

"It's okay, Branna," Julia whispered. "I remember."

"You do?" Branna pushed herself up on her arm and turned Julia to face her. "Everything?"

"No, not everything. Not yet. I can feel it at the edges of my mind. Like remembering a dream, but the harder I think about it, the hazier it all becomes again, and..." Julia pinched the bridge of her nose and sat up on the side of the bed. "...I get this stabbing pain behind my eyes."

"So, how much do you remember?"

"I know we weren't alone. I know it was Captain Shaw. I thought he was you and he touched me." Julia ran a finger down the side of her face.

Branna's hands clenched in anger, wishing she had been the one to end his life. "Julia, I'm so sorry I didn't believe you."

"I was so out of it, even I didn't think he was real at first. He said I would be dead soon and that he had come for me. That we belonged together."

Branna felt rage building inside her at Julia's recounting. All this had happened right in front of her, and she had done nothing to protect Julia. "What else?"

"I know how you found me. On deck, raving like a madwoman and lunging at shadows. I wouldn't have believed me either. You did the only thing you could." Julia hissed a breath, her hand going to her head.

"Julia." Branna reached for her.

Julia moved off the bed and splashed water on her face from the wash basin. "I'm sorry but you distract me. I need to remember what happened or I'll never be able to move on."

Branna swung out of bed. "You don't have to do this all at once."

"I killed him, didn't I?"

Branna's lips pressed together into a thin line. "Aye. I believe so."

Julia searched for her clothes, pulling on the nearest she could find and stepping into her boots.

"Where are you going?" Branna hurried to get dressed.

"To the *Windswept*." She threw open the door and rushed out.

"Julia, I'm so pleased to see you up," Genevieve said as Julia raced down the stairs.

"Slow down," Branna said, thundering down behind her.

Genevieve stepped in front of them at the bottom. "What's going on?"

"Julia wants to see the *Windswept*. She's remembered a lot of what happened but some of the details are hazy," Branna said.

"Right now? Maybe you should wait until you feel a bit better." Gen looked Julia over with concern.

"I need to know, Gen. I need to know he's dead this time and for that I need to remember."

Genevieve pursed her lips. "I'll come, too."

"Captain!" Jack called as he ran into the courtyard and skidded to a stop in front of them, breathing heavily.

"What is it, Jack?" Branna barked, not even trying to hide her exasperation at the interruption.

"Thomas Blythe is back and down at the repair yard demanding to get aboard the *Windswept*."

"Bloody hell. Not now." Branna knew this was coming, but she thought she'd have more time to decide how she wanted to deal with him. Her main concern was Julia and he was in the way. Again.

"What the 'ell is goin' on?" Merriam grumbled, the increasingly loud conversation drawing her attention.

Julia pinched the bridge of her nose and squeezed her eyes shut. "I'm going to the ship. I'll talk to Thomas Blythe. The rest of you can come or not."

The lane to the repair docks was streaming with people and even lined with vendors. It seemed the entire marketplace had relocated out here. Julia hadn't made it very far before she staggered under the onslaught of noise, smells, and jostling of people.

"Julia, wait!" Branna shoved her way through the crowds to get to her, trailed by Jack, Genevieve and Merriam.

"What is this? What's going on?" Julia blinked and looked around.

Branna slid an arm around her waist and pulled her close. "It's the *Windswept*."

"Bugger me!" Merriam blurted. "This is mad."

Even the usually unflappable Genevieve was wide-eyed. "It's like the second coming."

The crowd grew even more dense as they neared the docks and the rumble of conversation, shouts of excitement, and the funk of booze and sweat hung thickly in the air.

A rough wooden barrier had been erected along the waterfront to keep gawkers from trying to sneak aboard the ship. It was manned every few feet by one of the *Banshee* crew to keep the crowd back and allow the repair crews to do their job. The dock was bustling with workers clearing away refuse and rotting lumber to make way for new parts and wood, and a fire burned in a large iron brazier on the dock, heating tar for construction.

Branna's eyes swept the area for any sign of Nat and Gus while keeping a tight grip on Julia. She didn't want them to get separated. There was tension around Julia's eyes and her posture was coiled and tight like she was ready to flee at any moment. Before Branna had a chance to check in with her a shout from the barricade drew her attention.

"Get the fuck outta my way, Hawke!" Thomas Blythe's voice boomed over the crowd. "This is my ship!"

"Back off, Blythe," Gus snarled back.

"Not by the laws of sea salvage," Nat said, his voice measured. "This ship and all its contents belong to Captain Kelly."

"Come on." Branna pulled Julia toward the front of the crowd, weaving her way through and leaving the others to fend for themselves.

"Fuck her!" Thomas Blythe roared. "And fuck you, too!"

Branna cleared their way through the crowd and crossed the barricade in time to see Thomas Blythe charge Nat and Gus. He was obviously drunk, and they put him down easily, with an arm jerked up high behind his back. He struggled and screamed his rage into the dirt while Gus held him down.

Julia pulled her hand from Branna's and drew closer. "You're hurting him."

Nat put an arm out to stop Julia from getting closer. "Stay back, miss."

Branna put a hand on her shoulder. "Julia, I'll handle—"

"No." She flinched away and glared at Branna. "Let him up."

"Captain, he's drunk and dangerous," Gus said, keeping Blythe pinned to the ground.

"He's not dangerous. He's grieving." Julia crouched down next to Blythe. "It's going to be all right, Mr. Blythe. They're going to let you go, now."

He could do little, but nod in agreement.

"Let him go, Mr. Hawke," Branna said, trusting Julia's instincts.

Blythe shook out his shoulder and glared at Branna. "That's my ship, Kelly."

"I don't necessarily disagree, Mr. Blythe, but for the foreseeable future it is in my custody."

His eyes narrowed. "I demand to be allowed—"

Branna bristled at his continued hostility. "No one goes on that ship without my express permission."

"Branna," Julia said and bent to her ear. "He needs to know what happened, or he'll never be able to move on. You can give him that. It's time."

Branna understood. She could end this for him. For them both. "Mr. Hawke, bring me the *Windswept*'s log."

Gus didn't have to go far. There was a stack of salvageable personal effects on the dock waiting to be returned to the appropriate friends and family members. Gus retrieved the log and handed it to Branna.

Branna turned it over in her hands before passing it to Thomas Blythe. "This should answer some of your questions."

Thomas Blythe took the book with trembling hands, the fight going out of him as he was faced with the truth of finding out what happened to his brother and his ship and crew. He tried to flip through the clumped and damaged pages, swearing in frustration when the damaged pages tore.

Julia placed her hands over his to stop him from tearing it more. "I'm sorry it's so damaged. We tried to be careful with it. I understand how badly you want answers, but you'll have to go slow. Your brother was a hero. I'm sure you knew that already. Now everyone will." She carefully turned the pages to where the entries about the *Windswept*'s stop for repairs and exploration of the island began. "Start here."

"When you're ready, Mr. Blythe. Come find me and we'll discuss the *Windswept*'s future," Branna said.

He made a strangled sound, his throat working and muscles jumping in his jaw, but no words. He tucked the logbook under his arm, bowed his head and hurried away through the crowd.

"Bloody hell," Branna muttered as she watched him disappear. When she turned around Gus and Nat had moved off to break up a drunken brawl and Julia had slipped away. She searched the crowd. Merriam and Genevieve were talking with Jack just down from the barricade. "Where did Julia go?"

"I thought she was with you," Genevieve replied.

Branna whirled around again and looked down the dock. She was there, wending her way past the lumber and equipment, avoiding the workmen and staring up at the ship which floated just a few yards from the dock.

Julia headed down the dock, carefully avoiding tools, workers, and stacks of lumber, never taking her eyes off the ship. She didn't know what she expected to feel but was surprised to remain so calm. She eyed the ship with detached interest. In the daylight, with all the life and activity around her she looked very much like the *Banshee* but older, more worn, and somehow, sad. As if, given the ability to share her story, she would weep with the telling of it.

The sinister mystery, haunting sounds, and horrific stench were all gone, replaced with hammers and saws, and the smell of fresh-cut wood and burning tar. The heat of the fire as she neared the hot tar stopped her and she gazed into the low flickering flames and red-hot embers. She remembered. Not the vivid memory of a brutal fight of a few days ago but the hazy, fleeting memory of a trauma long past.

Julia squeezed her eyes shut and massaged her temples as the pain in her head spiked for a moment then eased to a dull ache behind her eyes.

"Do you want to go aboard?" Branna asked from behind her.

"I don't think so. I think he wanted me to kill him."

"Why do you think that?"

"He could have killed us anytime and he didn't." She turned back to the fire and searched for the details. "I heard you fall through the deck and shout my name. I found the knife stuck in the deck. It was the only weapon I had, and I hid nearby behind some crates. He didn't look for me but waited for me to come to him, without saying a word."

"What happened?"

Julia grimaced at the memory of his grotesque features. "Despite his injuries I couldn't have put up much of a fight. He smiled as I stabbed him and slit his throat."

"Julia it was the only thing to do. If he welcomed death, then you did him a service. Showed him mercy and maybe gave him some peace. Please, let that knowledge give you some, too."

"There was so much blood," she murmured before clenching her hands into fists and sucking in a deep breath. "It's over. He's gone and that's all that matters."

"It's not all that matters, Julia." Branna took her hand, smoothing out her fist and lacing their fingers together. "What happened to us matters and how you feel matters. Are you okay?"

Julia took a deep breath and raised her brows at Branna. "What happens now? What are your plans?"

"I beg your pardon?" Julia was so good about talking about how she felt, especially when she was struggling with something, but it appeared she was already looking forward and not back. Whether that was a good or bad thing remained to be seen.

"Where does the *Banshee* sail next?" Julia asked.

"I think I would like us to decide together what we do next."

"Since when?"

Branna winced. Up until now she had never consulted Julia about her plans. She was the captain and she decided where and when the ship and the crew went. Julia chose this and chose to share this life with her.

Branna wanted things to be different, now. She wanted Julia to have some control over their next action. Julia was her heart. She was *the* heart. Julia was the strongest and most courageous person Branna had ever known. Julia knew her own mind so well and would never back down from confrontation, especially internal, no matter how painful.

It was Branna's hope that if she let Julia take the lead, she would know what to do to heal herself, and Branna and their friends would be there for her, whatever she needed.

"Well, it's about time that changed, I guess. What do *you* think we should do?"

Bella Books, Inc.

Women. Books. Even Better Together.

P.O. Box 10543

Tallahassee, FL 32302

Phone: (800) 729-4992

www.BellaBooks.com

More Titles from Bella Books

Mabel and Everything After – Hannah Safren
978-1-64247-390-2 | 274 pgs | paperback: $17.95 | eBook: $9.99
A law student and a wannabe brewery owner find that the path to a fairy tale happily-ever-after is often the long and scenic route.

To Be With You – TJ O'Shea
978-1-64247-419-0 | 348 pgs | paperback: $19.95 | eBook: $9.99
Sometimes the choice is between loving safely or loving bravely.

I Dare You to Love Me – Lori G. Matthews
978-1-64247-389-6 | 292 pgs | paperback: $18.95 | eBook: $9.99
An enemy-to-lovers romance about daring to follow your heart, even when it's the hardest thing to do.

The Lady Adventurers Club - Karen Frost
978-1-64247-414-5 | 300 pgs | paperback: $18.95 | eBook: $9.99
Four women. One undiscovered Egyptian tomb. One (maybe) angry Egyptian goddess. What could possibly go wrong?

Golden Hour - Kat Jackson
978-1-64247-397-1 | 250 pgs | paperback: $17.95 | eBook: $9.99
Life would be so much easier if Lina were afraid of something basic—like spiders—instead of something significant. Something like real, true, healthy love.

Schuss – E. J. Noyes
978-1-64247-430-5 | 276 pgs | paperback: $17.95 | eBook: $9.99
They're best friends who both want something more, but what if admitting it ruins the best friendship either of them have had?

Printed in the USA
CPSIA information can be obtained
at www.ICGtesting.com
JSHW020326230923
48990JS00001B/2

9 781642 474596